And So I Took Their Eye

Ben C. Davies writes with precision, curiosity, and a willingness to get close to the nerve. In *And So I Took Their Eye*, he plays with form – his stories appear as letters, therapy notes, and fractured timelines – to track how vengeance plays out across countries and communities. The stories are tough, honest, and threaded with grace. Along the way, Davies defines his own voice in his homage to the shapes, tones, and rhythms produced by writers he loves.

Whether it's the priest in Bolivia, the British traveler hiding out at a yoga retreat in Mexico, or the daughter watching her mother seek quiet revenge over tea at an English cricket match, these are stories about what we carry, what we can't undo, and what lingers.

Matthew Clark Davison, Author of Doubting Thomas

Ben C. Davies' stories are arresting: the prose sharp and unrelenting, his characters' 'true colours' revealed with an arch wryness. Davies forces us to re-think all that we do not want to see – in our societies, in our cultures. Bravo!

Alicia J Rouverol, author of Dry River *and*
I Was Content and Not Content

Few short story collections have the richness and complexity of a novel. Ben Davies' does.

Edward Stanton, author of Frail Blood *and*
VIDAS: Deep in Mexico and Spain

And So I Took Their Eye

Ben C. Davies

Bridge House

British Library Cataloguing in Publication Data
A Record of this Publication is available from the British
Library

ISBN 978-1-914199-96-7

This edition published 2025 by Bridge House Publishing
Manchester, England

Cover illustration © Natàlia Pàimes

For Kiki & Elio

Contents

Author's Note

This collection was first inspired by something awful that happened to someone I knew in Guatemala. It was driven by the adage, 'an eye for an eye' – a way of thinking that is still very much a part of daily life there, which calls for exact retaliation for a crime.

Upon completing it, I thought more broadly about the complex relationship between revenge and justice, and how these ideas show up in different cultures and societies. That reflection pushed me to explore these themes on a global scale, writing stories that cross borders and shed light on the many ways vengeance, retribution, and justice play out.

As the collection grew, the stories connected, revolving around a core group of characters who appear and reappear throughout. While each story stands on its own, together they form a larger, interconnected narrative. In this way, *And So I Took Their Eye* is both a collection of short stories and something closer to a novel.

The writing draws heavily on the work of Latin American authors, including Selva Almada, Javier Zamora, and Fernanda Melchor. Their work inspired not only the thematic depth of the collection but also stylistic choices, including the deliberate omission of traditional speech marks in some stories.

This book is also a response to the rising tide of hate and fear we're seeing worldwide – people shutting out immigrants, refugees, and the unhoused, driven by the racist, xenophobic rhetoric of a select few. I wanted to create something that pushes back against that, however small, offering a voice of empathy and welcome.

A Gringo Died Today

Hammock swinging, baby sleeping. Mosquitos buzzing and grains of black sand on the concrete floor. Church music blaring and Don Miguel's morning cough ticking like a clock. A new day like all the rest.

Rising from your sheets though, you notice how your sweat tastes different this morning. Salty not sweet. Your shirt slapped down sodden, a change from the usual crumpled mess. Beside you Claudia is still asleep, so that's normal. She'll have been up all night with the little one whilst you again snored through. Looks the same as ever, her thin traces of beauty smudged by years of tortillas and frijoles. "Reina de belleza" they said, though now you'd do well to see it. Turning out just like her mamá, though she wouldn't be the first. A shame, though she'd say the same about you. Worse even. Drink like your papá too, which was something you promised you wouldn't. A lifetime of broken promises, though at least you gave her a kid and she's happy it's a girl even if you're not. Maybe it's a good thing your family line ends here. The only good one was your hermana Juana, but she got out long ago, all the way to the land of the free. The rest of you, wastes of space to the end, especially the eldest, God rest his sad soul.

You move to stand and that's when the pain begins. Sharp and targeted, right to the forehead. Nothing new there, it's the same every time the sun pops up. You can taste the drink on your breath right away, hot and stale at the same time. No wonder Claudia can't stand to sleep close anymore though really, she gave up long ago.

You take a sip of Sprite from the glass bottle sat on the sweating floor, warm and flat yet it helps. The morning sugar rush more urgent than any café. As you lumber upright little droplets of sweat cloak your tubby body so you turn to the

9

fan for relief, yet it just spins dust straight back at you. Cheap like everything else in this dump you call a home. No place to bring up a kid, ¿but what other choice have you got? Poor little girl, waking up every day in this dog pit. The rich kids can never handle the rainy season so all roll away in their fancy cars with their blacked-out windows, but for your little one there's no choice. Just has to deal with days like today where the humidity pummels you despite the early hour. The only break is when the rains hit, but that just brings the mosquitos and whatever disease they're cooking up for the season, so it's the same shit served different.

Hoping for some kind of morning breeze you open the shutter and let your eyes wander out. Straight away you spy Walter selling fresh cocos to gringos from his front porch, his kids running scattered rings round his feet, giggling in the morning sun. You found out he sells the powder to the gringos now too. Cocos and cocaíne, someone's got to do it.

Now Claudia begins to stir, kicking sheets off in the process. She looks up, gives you an eye, and then shows you her back. You know that eye, seen it far too many times and it never gets easier. One that says you've done something wrong, something bad. What, you can't remember. Never can. The alcohol does that to you, it always has. You decide to face her later, easier that way, after you've had some more Sprite and something to eat, maybe even a morning cerveza.

The baby is still knocked out, rocking back and forth on the little hammock by the bed, so you slide out before she wakes even though you know it will spike Claudia's anger further. When she was born you promised you'd help out at home, but of course you don't. Yet another promise broken. The baby doesn't do much, ¿so what's there to do? Just sleeps, shits and cries. Hopefully you'll like her more when she can talk. Neri said that happened with his little girl, though he'll always be a better papá than you.

Quietly you take a step out onto the concrete porch, the floor still fresh under the shade of your palm roof, and see Walter look up. He keeps your eye for a second but there is no normal morning greeting, no guilty laugh for the night before. Only a look, one you've never seen before, one you can't work out. Another new different, only you're too hungover to ask why. You can deal with Walter and Claudia later, it's already time for that drink.

You slide on your sandals, the thin soles breaking through to the ground below, and stagger down the dust track towards Luis's tienda. His speakers fight against the church's, a horrid clash of noise that only makes your headache worse. That song too.

Siempre te voy a querer, Me aseguraré de enamorarte cada día.

Always the same fucking song on repeat, no wonder no-one likes drinking at his anymore. Luis is the same as usual though, reaches for the Sprite before you even ask. You throw some quetzales down and take a seat on one of the red plastic chairs, all branded in the bright red of Gallo beer. They'll take over the whole village before long. Them, the rich kids, and the gringos.

See, one day it was your village, the village you'd always known with the same families and faces for generations, probably too close in relation at times. Then snap, everything changed. Suddenly white faces were everywhere, busloads of people charging in, Semana Santa a never-ending party covering the beach in trash. Some locals say they like the change, but it's only because they're the ones making the money. For everyone else it's a nightmare you all saw coming.

Beauty can only stay beauty for so long before greed takes over and turns it all to shit.

Your abuela said that, minus a few words. She'd seen it

11

happen all before up north, the same sad reality on repeat. Busy and drunk and loud and dirty and full of girls in tiny bikinis that only make you mad because you've never got a chance with any of them, and anyway you're stuck with Claudia. The sleepy fishing town with the village fairs and the school parades and songs at Navidad all long gone.

¿And for what? It's not like the new people from the city or the gringos treat any of you with respect. The opposite in fact, looking down on you because you've worn the same shirt for three days straight and it stinks of sweat, but only because you've spent every day out in the angry sun building them a second home for shit poor wages. Looking down on you even though you were all born on the same earth. The only time they like you is for a photo, flicking out their fancy camera phones to take a snap of another poor person living under a palm roof. Good for their social media or whatever it is they do. It's enough to make you give up.

A gringo died today.

Luis machetes your thoughts in such a direct way that for a second you are taken by surprise and can't respond.

Brenda told me, he carries on. They found him on the shore, his body limp like weeds.

You take a sip of your Sprite. ¿Drowned?

Luis shrugs. Drunk probably, the sea is a cruel mistress.

You laugh but only because Luis has been saying that same line for years now. A gringa taught it to him and it must have stuck because he can't seem to say anything else. You take another sip and go to meet Luis's eye to ask more when a flicker of last night suddenly hits. It often happens this way after you drink, little stories revealing themselves as the day goes by. Snippets of memories you struggle to piece together.

You were here last night with the boys though, that

12

much you remember. Jorge, Julio, Walter, maybe Neri though his face is blurred. You were watching the football through the bars of the tienda, crushed cans of Brahva littering the floor. Julio was laughing, snorting too, and that's how you found out about Walter and his new line of work. Some gringos were there and drinking even heavier than you, no doubt on their way to the new beach club. Beach clubs in the village, who'd have thought. You're almost glad your abuela died younger than she should. Meant she never had to watch all her fears come to life.

One gringo had his back to you, but he towered above the rest. Wearing an oversized, sand yellow shirt, one way too hot for the humidity. Talking lots, animated, his hands always moving, even joined you all for a beer. Chatty guy, confident. Tried on his Spanish which was more than most. Took a few lines from Walter too, not a care in the world. It was lucky for some. Then another came over, a gringo you'd seen around the village, spoken to even, but then the memory ended, and you were right back to the now and Luis talking about the sea.

When he carried rambling on to discuss the always rising noise, you stopped listening. The problem with Luis is he never knows when to shut up. Unless you jump in, he can just talk and talk and talk. Another reason why everyone stopped drinking at his tienda and moved on to the new spots. That and all the bikini-wearing chicas. You still like Luis's place though, even if the music drags and he's a bore. It reminds you of the old times.

On that note your stomach churns and it's your cue. You leave without saying goodbye, shuffling away from the tienda towards Rosa's for some breakfast. This is another place that hasn't changed and the only one that never will. The city people and the gringos don't do well with all the flies and strays that join for dinner, always buzzing and barking and shitting, your hand forever flicking pests away. You don't mind though, means you never have to wait, the tortillas and frijoles on your plate before you have time to ask.

Buenos días mi amor.

You nod back a greeting.

¿You hear about the gringo?

You sigh, not in the mood for conversation. You love Rosa, another mother of sorts, but right now the hangover hurts. She can see that so slips some quetzalteca into your coffee to loosen you up. Not many people visit her these days, so she wants the conversation. Every week there's always a new story to tell, some better than the rest.

Last week it was all about some drama at the lake. For once there was a gringo at hers too, some fidgety kid called Archie. A name you'd never heard before and couldn't say right even when he tried to help. Him and you were sat there listening to Rosa, though the gringo was way more into it than you. All about a young girl that was assaulted and the guy who did it being hung in the street for all to see.

An eye for an eye, Rosa said, and the gringo repeated her word for word.

You were half listening then and you're half listening now. Taking it in one ear even if not responding. It's only when she says the next part that you give her your full attention.

The gringo was murdered they say.

You can't help but get sucked in. ¿Murdered?

That's what I heard, she replies, happy to have your gaze. Everyone in the village is talking about it.

¿How? Your curiosity piqued. ¿I thought he drowned?

Drowned on his own or drowned by someone else, Rosa replies calmly as if it was the most normal thing in the world.

Not for you though, as your mind is suddenly thrown to

14

the memory of your wet T-shirt on the floor and then it sparks something new.

You never go to the new places unless forced, especially the shining lights of the clubs, but you now remember you were there last night. You and the boys, shirts off, jumping up and down to some DJ wearing one of those bucket hats you see everywhere. The kind of shit your mamá made you wear as a baby that are somehow now trendy. He had a shitty goatee too and wore a stupid vest that said "Me Gusta Guatemala" in bold, funky letters. The guy was clearly on something, his eyes wonky, but in fairness his music worked. New to your ears but with the rum inside you, your feet were moving.

Now you remember the kid Archie was there too, alongside the gringo in the big yellow shirt, with some chica dancing saucily up on him. She was Guatemalan though not from the village. City type in a slinky red dress and her tits pushed up high. He looked over at you all and gave a silly wave, proud of himself. An arrogant grin on his sunburned face. Then he reached round and grabbed her ass tight and pulled the chica close.

She didn't like that one bit though, slapped his hand away and pushed him off, and you all cheered and laughed as she stormed away. The gringo followed her, apologising, pleading, and it was nice to see one of them look so pathetic. Then Walter appeared by your side, lifted the back of his hand to your nose and the memory fades into another blur.

Unlike Luis, you say goodbye to Rosa. She wouldn't let you not, though she doesn't charge for the breakfast. She rarely does these days even though she knows you must have some money 'cause you're always hungover. You'll pay her back one day, you owe her enough. The place you always ran to when your papá had had too much to drink

15

and his right arm was swinging. Huddled in the corner of your corrugated-iron shack before making a run for the door and racing down the street into the arms of Rosa. He would never follow you there, not to her house, which is exactly why you went.

In that moment you promise to not be the same as him and this is one vow you know you'll keep. Maybe the only one, but you will. And for a second you miss the baby even though you saw her an hour ago and she does nothing but sleep and shit and cry, and that feeling of missing her makes you happy because it might be the first time you've felt anything real towards her, and now all you want to do is go back home and be with her. But going back home means seeing Claudia and you're not ready for that yet, not while you stink of quetzalteca and your head still hurts, so you decide to head for the sea as there you can wash it all away.

Normally you go to the river, but that's too calm for a day like today. You need the waves to hit you, straight and hard to the face to smash the drink out of you. It's times like this you wished you still surfed as that was always the best cure. A morning out there on your board, joking and messing about with the crew. Flying down the face of monsters, your gut in your mouth, screaming in a joy even the drugs couldn't magic together. Barely drinking back then as you didn't want to be out too late because then you'd miss the best waves. How long ago that all felt now.

As the rum increased, the waves vanished. Then your belly got big, your board snapped, and you never got round to fixing it because you preferred to spend the money on drink. So it stayed out the front of your shack, a pathetic picture of lost dreams, until one day Don Sergio's kid asked for it. Now you see them out there surfing every day. Some say they might go pro whilst you haven't caught a wave since. Instead, all you can do is run against the wave, not

16

with it, let it hit you and pull you down and wash away the toxic waste inside you. It does a job. When you finally get to the beach though that option is immediately robbed from your slippery grasp.

The crowd is bigger than you think you've ever seen, even larger than Semana Santa when the parties are in. A swirling mass of bodies that frightens you because it's so foreign. Practically the whole village must be there, as well as the gringos and the dogs and the city people and the army and the police. People fucking everywhere and you just know the swim isn't going to happen and you've of course figured out why.

In the distance you spy the boys, Julio and Walter chatting away, hunched, and you walk towards them, but Walter pretends not to see you even if you know he does. He just snakes away and drags Julio with him and your gut confirms something is up. Something involving you though you don't know what.

You start walking through the crowd to find out, pushing the gringos aside until you get to an opening, a circle, wide and large with dogs running and barking in the middle. The police and some of the army guys are there too. The police who are new to town, brought in by the gringos. Decades of you all asking for a police station and nothing happens and then the gringos ask and one is built in months. Of course it is.

Next to the police you notice a few gringos who are crying. Men on their hands and knees, sobbing their eyes out in front of everyone. You watch them for a minute or two, curious, then decide enough is enough and get to leave, yet just as you turn you catch a glimpse of what they're bent over.

All you can see is a shoulder, but you know in an instant who it is. ¿How can you not? That big yellow shirt, the one

17

you can't escape from. The one that keeps the memories coming.

The water had covered you both. Clothes drenched including his big yellow shirt, hanging low off his lifeless frame. You were pulling him out from the sea, away from her claws, bringing him back to earth. On the beach you could make out some shadowy figures in the distance. Julio and Walter and Rodolfo, that Archie kid from breakfast at Rosa's, and some chica you sort of recognised. The dancing one in the red dress. She was crying and crying as you staggered your way out of the ocean, dragging the body with you, his yellow shirt painted black by the sand.

In the memory no one came to help, which you find strange. And then you remember the weight of it, the pure weight of the body. Worse than any bricks you lumbered around a site for some rich kid from the city. Every step hell as you dragged his body out, screaming, pulling him back to life.

When you got to the shore you threw his body down, though you didn't try to bring him back to life anymore. He was dead, you already knew that. The eyes had rolled, foam frothed at the corners of his mouth, and his lips had turned blue. Already so floppy that you were surprised he had once been a living and breathing animal and it was with that thought front and centre when you collapsed to the sand to join him.

You had curled up right next to the dead body, panting and panting and panting for breath. Sucking, clawing at any air you could find, thinking that maybe you were next, that the sea had done for you too, the cruel mistress, as Luis liked to say. And only then had your friends circled towards you. The gringo was by their side too as they huddled over both bodies. One dead, one nearly dead. The girl was no longer there, though you could hear her cries disappear into the distance as she ran down the beach, almost like an echo that kept going, going, going.

Then Julio bent down and asked, '¿qué paso?'

And for some reason he was crying too, but he also looked scared, the whites of his eyes shining like the full moon above. But you weren't scared, in fact you were the opposite.

Instead you had smiled, proud, and said, an eye for an eye, though you have no idea why. Then you had passed out.

When you woke a few hours later, everyone had gone. Just the stars sparkling up ahead, brighter than ever before. You could have stared at them for hours but then you saw what was lying next to you, still, just like your baby girl when she sleeps. The foam in his mouth had dried up by now, the little bubbles burst, and there was something so disgustingly peaceful about the whole thing, so innocent, that you had reached out your hand and traced the tip of your right index finger across the lines of his brow. Brushing the black sand out of his matted hair. Then reality had hit and you got anxious fast, unsure what to do.

And so you had ran. Sprinting as best you could across the beach, lit up by the light of the moon and the stars, stumbling in the sand yet always going forward. On and on, right back to the crummy little shack you called a home. And when you had got inside the baby was crying and wailing as if she knew something bad had happened. Claudia was awake too, trying to nurse the poor little thing, and she had glared at you and for some reason that look, that piercing judgement broke you, and you had started to cry. Shoulders slumped, nails clawing at your eyes as through those sobs you had then started to speak. Words coming out in pathetic bursts painted in tears, only you can't remember exactly what you said. Only that her reaction was first shocked, then sad, then angry and then scared.

And now you're right back in the moment, the morning sun beating down, and suddenly aware that one of the crying gringos is now pointing right at you. That twitchy guy with the funny name who had breakfast with you at Rosa's, now with his stubby, shaking finger aimed in your direction. The others you recognise from Luis's too, the boys who were drinking with yellow shirt, partying the night away, only they're not partying anymore. Instead they're pointing.

He did it, he did it, they start to yell, their fingers jabbing.

And the new police, the ones who have only just set up in town but act like they fucking own the place, start walking towards you. And suddenly everyone is staring right at you, including Julio and Walter who both look worried. And Claudia is at the beach too, clutching your little baby, looking even more worried than the rest, and you want to walk towards them, to be with them, but the police get to you first. They grab you by the arms, twist them behind your back, and pull you violently into the centre of the circle.

¿Are you sure? One asks in shitty English and the gringo with the funny name nods.

It was him, it was definitely him, he replies in shitty Spanish, his voice cracking, and all you can do is laugh.

You idiots, you cry. You point to the yellow shirted body on the floor and shout, I tried to save him. Loud for everyone to hear. I pulled him out of that bitch of an ocean and brought him ashore, but no one listens. No one believes you. No one even tries.

Instead, another gringo spits in your face and says, murderer, and the crowd starts to cheer. Your friends start to cheer. People you've known your entire life, but they're so scared shitless they'd rather stab you then save you. And you look to the police for help but nothing gives there and then the crowd gets louder.

You try to find Claudia but she is already gone, your dear baby girl with her. Only then do you start to panic. Only then does the fear start to gurgle up your throat and choke you, as the thought hits that maybe it's the last time you'll ever see your baby. That she is gone, and you'll never get to be the papá you promised you would be.

So you fight back, for her, rising from the floor to escape this horrid little moment, your fists begging, but the police stop you as quickly as you start. One takes out his gun and that's when you take the first butt to the face, knocking you straight to the floor. You hear the crowd cheer louder as they put cuffs on you and start to drag you away. Pulling you across the beach, your knees skimming across the sand. The crowd parts to let you and the police through, but the screams only grow louder.

Shame, they shout even though they have none themselves. Murderer.

And you try to explain to them all that they've got it all wrong. You scream out that you were trying to help, that you're no murderer, you should be the hero of this story. But no one listens, no one even tries.

And away you're dragged, right up the dune towards town, towards the station, knowing how this story ends. Yet it's as you're being pulled up the slope that you see it. Through the tear stains and the grains of black sand and the haunting cries, there you see it, caught in a patch of grass. Hidden, but you can still see it. Ripped at the side, lace and black, and you know you've seen them before.

You had left the party in good spirits. Rodolfo, Julio and Walter, and you. You made for the beach as you did at the end of every night. Rodolfo had picked up a little bit of weed from a gringo and you had wanted to watch the stars with a smoke. You were all laughing and giggling as you made your way there, before dropping down into the sand. Smiles on all your faces as you took your first drags.

You remember that feeling, straight after the first puff hits when the fog runs to your brain and you start to sink. The other three were chatting away, probably still high off the coke, but you went to a different space then. It was if your soul had drifted away from your body and was now looking down upon it. Then it started flying down the beach and you wanted to follow it. Feeling a surge of energy from somewhere you pulled yourself up and started swaying this way and that across the sand. Zigzagging along to the light of the full moon. It must have been a few hundred metres further down the beach, where all the hotels stop and it's just empty beach for miles and miles, when you heard it.

The boys were long gone now and it was just you and the sand and the moon and the hit of the weed and the crash of the waves and this noise. Muffled at first but there. A tiny little cry before a louder one, before another tiny cry. You stumbled towards it, your feet scuffing into the sand, following it bit by bit until the noise was right in front of you.

There, illuminated by nature above, the sound still fighting to be heard, you had seen yellow. That big, billowing yellow shirt, down, flat on the sand. At first you thought the gringo might be asleep but then you saw the shirt move. Up and down, up and down. You watched, confused for a second or two until you heard the same sound again and suddenly your brain focussed, and adrenaline kicked in. Your pupils narrowed and through a tiny gap between the yellow of his shirt and the nape of the gringo's brawny neck, you saw her little face.

Small, petite and beautiful, like Claudia once was.

Innocent eyes, clawing for help. The red of her dress now pulled up to her waist, ripped lace and black by her side. Then you heard her scream, heard her plead for mercy and that's when everything switched.

Without a thought you yanked out your belt, grabbed it tight in both hands, then swung it round the gringo's neck. Then with a roar you tore it back and his body came with it. Arched at the top before you dragged the belt to the left and the body crumpled into the sand. The girl immediately started scrambling to her feet, pulling her red dress down, her eyes saying gracias again and again even if no words came out.

You smiled at that, feeling good for something in your pitiful sad life. Feeling proud. Thinking again that you might be a good papá and you'd turn things around with Claudia and you were suddenly so happy at that thought, so taken by the whole idea, that you didn't notice yellow shirt loom up in front of you and his white fist swing into your face.

You took the hit hard. That mixed with the alcohol and the weed sent you to the floor. Hand to eye you tried to get back control and for a second you were worried, yet only for a second.

Your eyes had darted over to the gringo and there you found a broken state far worse than your own. Hands to his neck, desperately panting for breath and that's when you knew how this was going to play out.

You had grinned the next time he came at you. Ready, patient, in full control, as you rolled down into the sand to dodge his attack, then pounced upwards and hit him from below. See, this gringo might look sculptured on the outside, with his broad shoulders and model height, but he wasn't like you, he hadn't learned how to take punches, hadn't learned how to fend off a drunken papá from before

23

he could make a tortilla. The two of you were like one of Don Miguel's cockerels who fight for quetzales on a Tuesday night, pecking and clawing at each other in the pit. And there's always one cockerel who's so much better than the rest and you were that one on the beach, dipping and ducking and swinging and the gringo didn't know how to respond.

A fury had taken hold, a blind fury and you knew it wouldn't ever end as you thought, ¿what if that was your daughter? Your little girl who you now want to protect, who you now want to love and be good to, and you thought that when you hit him again. By then you were both in the water, in the cruel mistress, and fighting there in the crashing waves, and you knew it was game over.

This was your playground, you rode these waves before most could walk. Even in the dark you knew them better than you knew your own baby. Booming down harder and louder now because it's the season for rain, and in those crashing waves he came at you again but it was almost too easy by then. The lumbering gringo in his heavy yellow shirt. He knew he'd lost but he couldn't stop coming at you and that's when you had a decision to make.

You could take him to the shore now, pin him down and tell the new police in town all about it. That's what they'd do in Germany or England or one of those countries they say are civilised. But not here.

You knew they'd do nothing about it. She might be a rich Guatemalan, but she wasn't a gringa and the hierarchy went that way. As to your own word, well it was as good as shit. A drunkard, good-for-nothing builder against the gringo with the gym toned body and the expensive yellow shirt. And so you had another decision to make but in truth, it was something you'd made peace with ever since you saw the girl in the red dress fighting on the sand. A decision

24

stamped into the sand all because of what Rosa told you last week.

The story you'd half listened to then but couldn't have been clearer in your brain then. Of what happened up at lake amongst the volcanos and the sunsets and the water that goes till your eyes can't see any more. Of the young Guatemalan girl and the old gringo guy. Apparently he was well liked in the community but that wasn't enough. An eye for an eye, as the old saying goes.

It was your daughter, your Princessa, you thought of when you had pulled him down under the waves, his arms flailing in the air for help. You thought of her and Claudia and how proud they would be, protecting them from these pieces of shit. And even though you're a piece of shit you're not like this gringo, you could never do what he did and he deserves to go for it because there would be no justice otherwise. There never is in this place and so justice is for you to take into your own hands. And so you did.

By this point you'd noticed the boys on the shore, the gringo from Rosa's and the chica in the red dress by their side. They were all shouting and screaming and you'd figured they were cheering you on. She must have told them what happened and that gave you a new energy, stronger and stronger, able to hold him down despite the gringo's size and strength. And still they had made noise from the shore, so you realised that you needed to take them the body, to show the girl what you'd done, for her to thank you even.

So you held him and held him and held him, giving it everything you'd got, your biceps wailing against his endless assault for life. The dream to live still burning inside him, a flame whispering at the wick. Soon though, the arms stopped swinging and the body fell limp in the toing and froing of the waves, the yellow of his shirt the

25

only thing visible above the surface. Then you had turned the body round and that's when you saw that the eyes were gone, rolled back and lost to the murky waters below and you knew that justice had been served.

It was there that the memories merged together. The girl was no longer there, though you could hear her cries disappear into the distance, but the boys were, including the twitchy gringo.

Julio had bent down and asked, ¿qué paso? And he was crying but he also looked scared and so you had turned to face him, and Walter, and Rodolfo and the gringo Archie.

And there, when they were all close, all you could say was an eye for an eye. Then you collapsed deep into the sand and passed out.

Collapsed to the floor like you collapse to the floor now, only now you don't collapse to the soft black sand that had met your feet every single morning of your sad little life. Instead it's to the piss-stained concrete of a cell and you're spitting blood and one eye can't open. You try but it just won't open and you know it's fucked and you're not getting it back.

The guard outside the cell turns to look in but just smiles when he sees you and another quickly joins him. They tell you it's an international news story and you believe them. A gringo's blood earns a different kind of weight. And that makes you think of your family, your little precious family, and that maybe Claudia and your girl are better off without you anyway. That you were never going to change, and you'll always be a drunk good-for-nothing like Claudia says. But at least you did one thing right, one thing you can be proud of, one thing to make your little girl's life better and maybe she'd come find you one day, to thank you, congratulate you even. Or maybe she won't because you'll probably already be dead. You're not sure if you care anymore anyway.

26

That's when the door to the cell is opened and the guards walk in. One, two, three, four. You try to stand up to face them, but your legs can't do that anymore. That's when you notice your knee is out of joint too. You've got so much pain all over it's hard to tell where exactly it's coming from and that thought makes you laugh even though it isn't funny. And then the butt of the rifle hits and again you fall and when you fall it's not Claudia you think of or your little girl or Rosa or your big sister Juana or your papá or your boys or the girl in the red dress or even the gringo in the yellow shirt. Instead, it's the ocean.

The cruel mistress rearing up at you like a heron about to push off into flight, hanging there in front of you, taunting you, calling you in and so you step forward and that's when she crashes down on you and swallows you whole.

The Eagle of the Desert

The roof won't last the rainy season.

Eagle has been told this so many times by now I'm not sure why Loco still bothers because we both know Eagle won't budge, he never does even on the most trivial of things which is exactly why I find myself having to call a forty-four year old white man with long greying hair tied into a bun, Eagle, instead of his actual name even though I hate myself for doing so, but I figure what's the point in fighting it?

The man is as stubborn as they get and won't hear anything otherwise, so why not give the man what he wants? Especially when I consider what it takes to do the kind of life transformation that he's done, because Eagle's name is actually Dwight Jackson from Lincoln, Nebraska, but a spiritual leader called that, not to mention the Republican parents and siblings in the military, doesn't have the same ring to it, so Eagle it must be.

Not that he's told me any of his backstory of course, we've never delved hand-in-hand into his troubled family history, it's just what I found out one morning as I went down rabbit hole upon rabbit hole trying to work out how the hell I had ended up at this rural yoga retreat in the Mexican desert working for a man called Eagle, riled up in a permanent state of restrained fury which is exactly the opposite of what I set out to achieve and in fact was only making everything I'd been through worse than I could have imagined, because I was meant to be here to escape, and to get over something awful that happened on the beaches of Guatemala.

I had just needed some peace, some time to get my head in order, to get some clarity, for what I'd seen and what I'd done, instead of heading home, tail between my legs, back to little old England to explain to Mum and my younger brother Yorkie what had happened, because I wasn't ready for that, and I certainly wasn't ready for Mum's inevitable lecture, one she'd no doubt been holding on to ever since I left.

I told you so Archie. I told you. You never should have gone to that country. The government tourism guidelines said it was dangerous and just look what's happened. Scarred for life you'll be, I knew it, I knew it.

No, I couldn't take one word of that, I'd needed some time just for me, so it all seemed perfect when one morning I was scrolling my way through social media and this opportunity flashed up to work at a retreat offering 'solace, restoration and peace in a place of ancient, natural beauty' only I've got no solace, restoration or peace and the place might be ancient because every spot of land on this earth is ancient but it certainly wasn't a natural beauty, in fact it's the opposite.

Just a harsh, dust-flamed desert that sparks up a whirlwind of coughing in me whenever it likes, impossible to escape unless you're in your bedroom which isn't in fact a place to relax and unwind as promised, but a ten-bed wooden bunker that offers no ventilation or respite from the heat. A heat that pounds down every minute of the day until the only thing I can do is head outside and go to Eagle's sprawling new yoga deck with its unstable roof that's completely unnecessary for the number of people who attend this retreat and a stupid waste of money. Only built as some kind of laughable statement towards the new yoga retreat that's opened ten minutes down the road, the one I wish I'd applied to or could move to but I can't because Eagle cannily signed me up for six months work before I arrived. A legal move that seems out of place from a self-proclaimed free-thinking, free-spirit but I've accepted that

Dwight from Nebraska always bubbles under the surface so as a result I'm stuck, a state of play I regret more with every passing day.

All I can do is dream, imagining a different reality where I break the cursed contract, rip it up in a frenzy, my fingers tearing it into tiny little shreds before I run across the desert to the local town and scream, *let me in, let me in, I can't take this anymore, I can't take one more second of this, the embodied living and the divine power and the energy healing and the sensual liberation and the somatic healing,* and God-knows what else because I don't even know what half those things mean, but all that is just a pathetic little dream anyway, something I can't bring myself to do because I'm not built that way, so I stoically suffer instead, that stiff-upper lip bred deep.

The funny part is all I ever wanted was just a little bit of downtime, to get over what had happened on the beach, and, because I liked yoga and had downloaded Headspace on me iPhone, I thought this place made sense. That's all it was, yet now I'd do anything to be in that local town with some cold beers and a game of pool and a jukebox blaring out some fresh tunes because of course none of those things are allowed in the *Yoga Oasis*, a name that annoys every time I have to say it out loud because according to the dictionary an oasis means 'a fertile or green area in an arid region', yet there is absolutely nothing that is fertile or green about this place and the only person who is truly blind to that is Eagle, a man too busy flapping his wings at the locals, telling them what to do instead of listening to their words.

People who have lived on this ancient land far longer than he so you'd think he might appreciate that they know a thing or two, but Eagle doesn't see it that way and nor do any of the other employees who, for reasons I can't begin to fathom, lick the mud-crusted toes and thick-soled heels of his hairy feet. Feet that seem not to have ever seen sandals, let alone socks, and smell worse by the day yet none of the other employees seem to mind, in fact most do the same while they do their embodied living or whatever made up thing is on the calendar for that day, often just two words put together they say has meaning but I can't find it.

So instead I gravitate towards Loco and his crew, a more natural fit as with them I can have a laugh and sneak a beer whilst the others spend an hour every afternoon in meditation followed by an hour of chanting led by Eagle, which I obviously can't bear to be near, all under the shade of the new yoga deck with its huge roof which opened two weeks ago to great fanfare and lots of social media, purely to spite the yoga retreat down the road.

Naturally I was forced along to the opening party, the day that really cemented my hatred for Eagle, and the first time I properly met Loco and his crew. They had all brought along a few beers because it was a party, though they didn't know what an Eagle-organised party was, and as they were sat sipping their beers and sharing some laughs under the shade of the yoga deck roof, a roof they had constructed in the roaring heat, Eagle stormed over and reprimanded them all. Shouted at them to keep it down and that they were ruining the party and some weird form of silent expressionist dancing he was leading.

I nearly said something there and then. I felt I should have but I didn't because the last time I spoke up on the beaches of Guatemala things went south quick and as far as I could see there was nothing I could really do about it. Also, I wasn't in the mood to cause trouble because I had four more months on the horizon, four months of Eagle and his unbearable, ego-driven ways, so I had kept quiet for my own sanity and accepted the belittling then like I did the next day and the next for all the various supposedly awful things I had done wrong around the retreat, from bookings to cleanings to maintenance, wishing it all to end right until now, the moment Loco said would come.

The first of the summer rains hit slowly at first before building in density, in ferocity, in power, the storms Eagle was warned of which makes it all the more satisfying that they were now here, because Loco really had told Eagle again and again the roof was built too big, warned him, pleaded with him, tried to make him see reason but that Icarus was soaring way too high, no ear for the common man, so in the end something greater than man had to make him listen.

Eagle slips in the mud when the puddles start to form, a hilarious foreshadowing of what is to come, because then when the winds follow, swirling and rolling their way across the desert until they join forces with the rain in a spectacular, beautiful cacophony of energy, the rain starts to swamp the centre of the roof, a puddle that grows into a lake, building the weight on the roof up, up, up, until down, down, down the roof of the yoga deck falls and whilst Dwight from Nebraska slumps to his knees in a puddle of salty mud and tears, I kick off my shoes and begin to dance under the spray of the rain, timidly at first until it all lets loose, wilder, crazier, without thought, without rhythm, without insecurity or shame, finally finding what I'd been looking for, letting it all out as my feet splash through the water twirling this way and that, bouncing and spinning and jumping and laughing, and only then do I start to feel some sort of solace, some restoration and ultimately, some kind of peace in this ancient, natural beauty.

Teatime at the Cricket

In Guatemala they believe in the ancient saying 'an eye for eye', and after a poor woman was assaulted on one of their black sand beaches, a local murdered the American who did it and left him rotting there for all to see.

I'd never heard of Mayans or Guatemala even, but that's what Matty Lawrence told me as we stacked shelves at the Co-op one Saturday morning for £6.26 an hour. Matty, (who we called 'Yorkie' because he always seemed to have a bar of Raisin & Biscuit Yorkie on the go), went on to tell me, brushing his greasy highlighted hair back as he spoke, that his older brother Archie had been there on the beaches when it happened. This was part of Archie's famous gap year travels, something Yorkie told me about each and every time we stacked shelves, as if it was him doing all the travelling and not the older brother who I always thought was a show off.

When I told Mum about it later, she said it was Yorkie's way of flirting and he had a major crush. Well, if that's what he was doing he wasn't very good at it, because where his whole body bristled in this weird sort of excitement, my right ear started to twitch which only happened when I was really uncomfortable.

See, the way Yorkie explained the whole 'eye for an eye' thing was as if it was the most foreign thing ever, a faraway planet compared to the little English village where we lived. I didn't agree. He also added that pirates did the same thing and considering one of the people we learned about at school, the one who defeated the Armada and was a queen's best friend, was also a pirate, right out proved my point. (As a side note I also wondered whether that's why pirates had so many eye patches, though I couldn't find any confirmation of that theory.)

In England we obviously don't openly practice an eye for an eye like they do in this Guatemala. Even if our pirates did it and it was in the Bible, (which was something I later found out for myself as it turned out Yorkie didn't know all that much about an eye for an eye), it wasn't something you'd normally see on these shores. Especially round where I live where it's all strawberries and cream, scones and Pimms on the village green, and carols at Christmas. That kind of idea would shock the milk from the Earl Grey with the lot round here. Too vulgar for such well-mannered people. But that's only what they'd say. That's only what they want you to think.

We might not hang the rope round the old oak in the middle of green, yet the way I see it that same eye for an eye mentality bleeds through into every nook and cranny. I just didn't realise it until Yorkie shared his story. See in England, maybe even more than on the pirate ships or with the Mayans, we have this strict, rigid idea of fairness that dominates every part of life. Just look at the way we queue. Everything must be precisely fair, fairer than fair, or society crumbles. And crumble it did that long summer afternoon during tea at the local cricket match.

Mrs Thomas was on the teas that Sunday. Hands raised, I'd never liked Mrs Thomas, right from the first time I went to the cricket. It was if she was born into the roots of the little village where we all lived. That one day a tree was planted and out grew Mrs Thomas. Not a nice tree like the pines or willows I used to see on my walk to the Co-op. No, she was a different type of tree. Very much alive, but twiggy and sharp. Little elbows on the branches jutting out uncomfortably in all directions. It wasn't because of that I didn't like her though, she wasn't an old cranky type. In fact, she was the opposite.

Mrs Thomas was one of those who was so utterly friendly

to your face, smiling all the time, but I never believed her smiles. If she wasn't so dedicated to the cricket teas, I'd always thought she'd have been good in the village panto. What with her fake smiles and her 'Oh darlings' and her 'Dears', always putting on a show. As it was, she wouldn't be seen dead in a pantomime because the women dressed as men and the men as women, and that didn't sit right. At least that's what I heard her say to Mr Booth, left arm bowler and last Christmas's Widow Twankey, one afternoon at the cricket.

The teas were on a rota and every month she did one and so did Mrs Dorris and so did Mrs Knowles and so did Ms Hall (or B as Dad and I called her, 'cause B also happened to be my dear mum). Unlike the other three ladies who seemed to live for doing the cricket teas: the triangle-cut egg and cress sandwiches, the orange squash, the cucumber slices, the scotch eggs, the pork pies and the great Victoria sponge, my mum hated doing them. She proper hated it. Hated the pressure of it all, the precious little details of what was required, the pleasantries and the sucking up to the sweat clad men who swung their bats. She did it for my dad and because she loved being at the cricket, but as to the actual teas, she couldn't stand it. That was why she used to always bring me along too.

'H,' she'd say. 'Please love, be a good daughter now, would you? I can't stand being there alone. They'll be sniffing my sandwiches, especially that Mrs Thomas. Why can't they all just buzz off and go watch the cricket?'

See that's also how my mum was different to the other three. She actually loved the cricket. Loved it more than Dad even though he spent every Sunday morning preparing for the match (oiling his bat, knocking it in with an old red leather cricket ball, brushing dirt off his pads), then every Sunday afternoon playing the game (which often ended with a scratchy score of less than twenty and maybe a catch), and then every Sunday evening moaning or grumbling about the game he just played (or telling us on an endless loop about his catch or runs or whatever slightly noteworthy thing he did). Of course he liked cricket, but not like Mum.

Mum could watch every ball. Not just when Dad was in but every single ball. She was entranced by it, loved the whole song and dance of it all. 'Poetry' she called it, though I never really understood why.

This was even more surprising because Dad had been the one who had grown up playing it whilst Mum had never taken any notice of the sport until she started with Dad. I don't think she knew a smidge about it until one afternoon he asked her along to watch.

From the second she saw all those clean white kits peppered across the green turf, the cute pavilion with the outdoor loo, the little boys in their oversized knitted sweaters nervously waiting to bat, the balls lost to the neighbours' thorny hedge and the beefy old drinker from the pub swinging and swishing his willow around, she was in love. It wasn't normal for someone of her background, someone of her pronunciations. That's maybe why she was so smitten. The gentlemanly nature of it all was so far removed from her old place that it put a mirror up to her new life and gave her a reflection she liked.

It took me a good while to also realise that's exactly why they sniffed her sandwiches so hard. See if Mrs Thomas was one kind of tree, my mum was another and the most beautiful of all. She had these tiny, sculptured hands that could have won awards, fierce peroxide blonde hair, cropped and angular yet striking, great wide green eyes and a smile that could fire up any pub in the county. As you can imagine this was in complete contrast to all the bookish, large-gummed ladies who hobbled their way to the cricket, especially the three making the teas. And they didn't like that. Not one bit.

Now as I said at the beginning, the English love fairness and even if my mum was so crazily different to all the others, she was the same when it came to fairness. I think that can be the only reason why she did what she did. Even if she would never admit it, eventually it got to her. She was only human. How long can any person take a room going silent when you walk in, sniggers at your outfit, titters at the way you speak, turns up noses at your egg cress, and makes pointed suggestions when you chat to any man?

To her it was unfair and she, like every other person in town, liked fair. She knew exactly why they were doing it, even if I didn't at the time. Mrs Thomas, Mrs Dorris, Mrs Knowles to name just a few. Hungry mouths always twitching. Prodding and probing, niggling down into her earlobes like some irritating old pop song that never left the Roberts radio.

And I felt that unfairness with her every time, even when I didn't properly understand. When Mum felt slighted, I felt it too. I just took it different. They always said I popped out more like Dad which makes sense; he was a weak one at heart. Mum though, she was a wild thing and I loved to watch her in full flow, even if it was tensed up and through my fingers. And that was what I did when it all happened, through my fingers, jaw tight and my right ear twitching.

It started the last Sunday of June, the crescendo that is, though it had been building for a proper amount of time. It was just that last Sunday when Mrs Thomas finally went for Mum's eye, so to speak.

Mum was doing teas that day and Mrs Dorris was busying herself this way and that, pouring out the blackcurrant squash as if she'd paid the £1.25 a bottle and not Mum. One of the fast bowlers took a glass, another individual I didn't really like. He was tall and skinny with these beady little glasses and a thick moustache sat above his lip. Anyway, this bowler lifted the plastic glass to his lips for a sip and then promptly spat it all out, sprayed right across the cheap cream carpet below.

Mrs Dorris was on him in a flash. She bolted to his side, hand clasped round his shoulder, and said, 'Oh, I'm so sorry, Ralph, she always makes it too weak.'

Out of nowhere Mrs Thomas then arrived to add, 'Can you blame her? Must be second nature considering. Lasts longer that way.'

And I didn't really know what that meant, but Mum went bright crimson and shot for the exit, which was her way of saying it wasn't fair. I could tell it really hurt her, deeper than I could understand, but she never said a word about it. In fact I'd almost forgotten until two weeks later when Mrs Thomas was on the teas. That's when Mum decided to put into action Yorkie's little story. That's when I learned what an English eye for an eye was.

Our team was 164-8 when it all kicked off. This meant that the opposition team only needed two more wickets before everyone could run off for a break and Mrs Thomas's neatly prepared teas.

In hindsight I can see why Mum waited till then to do what she did. At the start of the innings all the older batters are in whilst the younger ones, often the sons of the older batters or the kids with bright dreams, were left to do the scoring of the match. Studiously writing into the scorebook like it was an end of year exam, terrified to make a mistake and stir the anger of the older men. By later in the innings though, this has changed. All those kids must go out to bat and the dads who are now out are meant to take over the scoring. The only problem is they're often too riled at being out, throwing bats and gloves and pads all around the changing room, to want to do it. That's where Mum would step in.

Mum loved to score, in fact she was brilliant at it. The second she hopped over to that old table, thin plywood pealing at its edges, and perched on the end of her rusty old chair, she would transform into a cricket scoring master. This meant she would not only jot down her own team's score but would offer and was trusted to do the other teams too. Admired even, apart from by the Thomas's and the Dorris's and the Knowles's of this world, who could only share their passive aggressive smiles Mum knew all too well.

Now if anyone knows cricket scoring they'd be sure to tell you it's incredibly complicated. I knew how to do it of course, Mum made it that way, but it was tricky. With every ball bowled the scorer has to mark down whatever happened in the batsman's column, then the bowler's, whilst also updating the overall score, and then transferring that to the weathered, black scoreboard behind, so all the players could see.

If it was no run you just marked down a dot which was relatively simple but if it was a run (1), or runs (2, 3, 4, 5, 6), or a no-ball (a circle), or a wide (a cross with dots added for any extra runs), or leg byes (upside down triangle with dots for runs), or the end of the over (chalking up everything and writing the new bowler down), or a worst of all a wicket (W, followed by the name of the new batter and updating the bowlers' figures), things got complicated quick. Everyone says cricket is so slow but when you're scoring it's the fastest thing in the world. You can't get distracted for even a second or you lose track dangerously quickly and then all hell breaks loose. Something Mum knew.

It was when the eighth wicket fell the chaos began. This

is often when cricket matches at this amateur level lose their militaristic structure. By now the bowling team is tired, disgruntled, and ready for tea. This only gets worse when someone's son walks out to bat. Everyone knows they can't bowl really fast at the young one because he's a kid and his dad is no doubt on the side-lines watching eagle eyed at every single ball bowled, and any fast one coming at his little boy is coming straight back at their young lad when the teams switch over.

So, a little game endures when not many runs are scored, a part-time spinner bowls what Dad calls 'twiddlers', and lots of dots are put on the scorecard. Everyone basically goes through the motions until the wickets eventually fall and they can all saunter off to some glasses of orange squash and Mrs Thomas's meticulous prepared tea. And when I say meticulous, I mean meticulous. She had already spent the first part of the game talking to Mrs Walters (wife of batsman number three and regular slip fielder Mr Walters) about how she'd prepared a few Marmite sandwiches specially for him as she knew they were his favourite.

Taking that all into account, by the time of the eighth wicket everyone was downright ready to go off, yet that was when little Freddie Wallace from the estate strolled out. All through my childhood I'd seen Freddie around, though we'd never been friends. Just nods in the park, that kind of thing. Last I'd heard he'd dropped out before GCSE's and was now apprenticing for his dad as a plumber. Freddie was a bit like Mum though. They'd clawed in the same childhood air, and she loved him for it. Proper adored him. I even got a bit jealous at times. He was new to cricket, all because Mum had seen him hitting a tennis ball with a slab of wood against a wall out the back of the butchers, and she thought he had something.

With Dad's help they'd gone down the cricket nets

twice a week for the last four months to teach him the game. Dad and Mum were both real vigilant about it (even at my expense) and now here was the end result, Freddie strolling out to bat.

Now to any classically trained cricket fan, Freddie was not your normal player. He had none of the required grace, as Dad explained. There'd be no late cuts, no cover drives, or sweeps from him (these are all cricket shots). All he had was something Dad called 'the eye'. A natural, unteachable skill to basically whack anything in the eye line. I'm not sure I've ever seen Mum or Dad more excited at a cricket match than when Freddie strutted out to bat. Even I was roped into the anticipation of it all, despite the fact I didn't really like cricket and I was still a little jealous of Freddie.

When Freddie's first ball was delivered a stunned silence swept over the entire ground. From the pavilion to the players to the well-mannered wives clustered on the boundary's edge. The bowler (who in true English fairness was being nice to the young lad who had walked out) saw the ball fly straight back over his head, one bounce and to the boundary rope. For the next bowl exactly the same thing happened. Two balls later, again. Always straight back over the head, I think it was the only shot they taught him. When the bowler tried one down the leg side to try and stop the attack, Freddie just took a step over and did it again. Now sweat was breaking out on all the fielders' faces as they realised tea was sailing off into the distance with every crunch of leather.

And that was exactly the moment Mum asked Mrs Thomas to take over.

As explained, scoring is hard at the best of times, but when the batters are scoring fast, it's even harder. Suddenly you're racking up the numbers, adding the batsman's score continually, and updating the scoreboard behind you with

41

every stroke. Mum was so skilled at it for her it was effortless, but for anyone else it was a tall order. So, when Mum asked Mrs Thomas to take over, she knew exactly what was going to happen.

By now everyone had gravitated to the boundary's edge to watch Freddie's relentless attack meaning Mrs Thomas, basically caressing her neatly cut sandwiches protected under cling film, was the only one around. Exactly, I think, as Mum had guessed.

'I need your help desperately,' Mum pleaded, a fake innocence to her tone. 'See, Freddie's mum asked if I could take some videos of him batting and I completely forgot when I started scoring and he could be out any ball. I just need to get one. Can you please take over the scoring? You'll be brilliant at it. I know how in-tune you are with everything that goes on here.'

With every 'but', 'what', stammer and question, Mum just kept assuring Mrs Thomas it would be all right, whilst giving a whistle stop tour of how to score. The buts continued however, so inevitably Mum turned to me.

'H, love, can you do the other team's score, just to help Mrs Thomas out?'

I didn't know what to say but yes, unsure as to what exactly was going on, other than it was something. But that was that and before Mrs Thomas could offer any more rebuttals, Mum was off, camera in hand, prancing down to the pitch with a twinkle in her eye. Mrs Thomas was left at the table with me plonked by her side, a mortified, stunned expression across her face.

Twenty-five minutes later the two teams walked their way to the pavilion for tea. Freddie strutted off, bat under his arm, helmet off, with 53 runs to his name. I'm not sure I've ever seen a wider grin. Not on his face mind you, which was the same cheeky grin as ever, but on Mum and Dad's (sprouting more jealousy inside of me). Then, as the players and their families moved in for tea, I noticed Mum skip her way to the scoring table and start innocently browsing the scorecard. A minute later, all hell broke loose.

'James,' Mum called to Dad. 'James, come and look at this.'

Dad quickly walked over, though I doubt he was party to anything Mum was doing. He always was a softer sort, all talk no action, the opposite of Mum. Anyway, as he moved towards her a large set of curious eyes quickly followed.

Mum then lifted the old leather-bound scoring book high into the air for all eyes to see. A book that has detailed every game for the last God knows how long. A book of honesty, decency and fair play, yet now used for another purpose entirely.

'See it says here Freddie scored eighteen in that over but in this scorecard, well, it says different. Here he only scored fifteen.'

Mum then dramatically walked over to the black scoreboard on the pavilion wall with the chalk-written numbers hanging from hooks upon it, drawing every eye as she went.

'See it says the total there is 221, but in this book it's 212.' Now her voice began to change, morphing into the well-mannered tone of the polite English women she so detested. 'I'm in all sorts of bother.'

What happened next were not scenes the English expected when they brought cricket to all corners of the globe. Maybe through their narrow-minded eyes it could be expected amongst the old convicts of Australia, or amidst the mayhem of Asia, but not in 'Good Old Blighty' as I often heard the wicketkeeper call it.

'B, what have you uncovered?'

43

That was the captain of Dad's team who now sauntered his way over to the table. He was one person at the cricket club I did like, with his swollen, hanging belly, his blotched cheeks and his big swinging cricket shots. He and Dad often went to The Bull late on a Sunday when I was all wrapped up in bed. Normally Dad's pub nights were enough to put Mum in a spin but when it was with the captain she never got angry because she liked him too. In fact, he was the only person she let call her B, other than Dad and me.

So now the captain was involved and as Mum started to explain, more people began to circle round the table, including an anxious Mrs Thomas. I saw Mum flash her the briefest, tiniest little smile, one that said a million unsaid things, before she took out a knife and went for her eye.

'See the scoreboard says our team have nine runs more than we got in this book and it wouldn't be right, it wouldn't be fair, it wouldn't be proper, if I didn't point it out. Don't get me wrong, I'd love those nine runs more than anyone. Heck that might lose Freddie his fifty.' She fake laughed now but it was only me who knew it was fake. 'But that's not right. One of these books is wrong and I don't ever want us stealing runs that ain't ours. That's just not cricket.'

'Stealing runs?'

The opposition captain now waltzed over, as every bit as smug in his delivery as you could imagine. This was an anecdote he could retell for years down the pub with every other cricket captain from the local area and he couldn't believe his luck. Not that the nine runs meant anything, but the insult to good old English fairness, now that was a story worth telling.

'I couldn't say for sure,' Mum continued. 'Janet?' She used Mrs Thomas's first name now, a brutal attack only a few of us could understand. 'Janet, what has happened?'

As Mrs Thomas began to stammer under the weight of

the allegations, a chorus of raised accusatory voices entered the scene.

'Why would I cheat?' she crowed defensively when the chorus grew louder. She then turned to Mum and pointed. 'Your daughter must have made the mistake.'

The brazen opposition captain laughed loudly, a hand to each hip. 'Bit convenient that it's the one who scored a lower total who made a mistake.' He then turned to me. 'Have you ever done the scoring before, dear?'

'Yes,' I mumbled back, my right ear twitching. 'I've helped Mum out lots of times. She taught me at home.'

The captain said nothing in return. Just opened his arms and shrugged, the same smug expression on his face.

Mrs Thomas now let out a small, restrained howl and looked to her husband for help. 'It makes no sense for me to cheat. Maybe I made a mistake. I don't know. Why would I bulk the scores? It's not like I want that little lout to score a fifty anyway.'

All eyes turned to look at Freddie whilst Mrs Thomas continued under her breath. 'Means he'll be coming back when he shouldn't even be here. It's not his sport.'

That part took Mum by surprise; you could see it in an instant. It wasn't part of the plan and it dared hurt someone other than herself, someone innocent, someone she'd dragged into the firing line. Not that I think Freddie understood or if he did, cared, but Mum was protective. Also I think more than that, the comment felt directed at her too.

It was about Freddie but they were peas from the same pod and Mrs Thomas knew that. She could direct her words at Freddie, but she was saying what she'd wanted to say to Mum since forever and this was her way of doing it. She knew full well where to throw her darts and this had hit a bullseye. An eye for an eye for an eye.

Mrs Thomas grinned viciously when she saw the

expression morph on my mum's face. What she did not account for however was that anyone hitting a fifty had a rare clout behind them not even the maker of teas could usurp.

'Now, now, Janet. None of that.'

'Bad form, really bad form.'

The shouts came thick and fast. Adult voices punctuated by Freddie's youthful cries, before it escalated. I'll never know if it was Mum who threw the first sandwich, but I do know who it hit.

Mrs Thomas took an egg and cress right to the face. At times I like to imagine it hit her right in the eye, but that would be pushing the truth. Wherever it hit, straight after all hell broke loose.

The smug opposition captain took Mr Walter's Marmite to the chin, smearing his white bristled goatee brown. Coronation Chicken at Mr Dorris shortly followed, before cucumber slices plastered their wicketkeeper's right cheek, Robinson's Orange Squash went over second slip, a Scotch egg went right into long leg's ear and Victoria Sponge went slap into the chest of mid-off. Little Freddie, unsure if this was normal or not, was loving every second and was soon throwing little carrots up in the air and using his bat to whack them right into the melee.

The opposition team never made it out for their innings. In fact I think it was the only game of cricket ever recorded in those red leather bound books to be cancelled because of a bad cricket tea. The only players who seemed not to care were Dad and the captain who now got to spend the afternoon in the pub.

Only this time Mum and I joined and laughed and laughed until that moment laughter dies and the captain turned to Mum and cheekily asked, 'So come on then B, let's have it out. You planned this all right from the start?'

To that Mum just winked, took a sip of her lukewarm house white, and then offered a cheers to Mrs Thomas' cricket teas.

Whose Story?

James enjoyed another healthy swill of his red, the crystal stem smudged by his tight grip. He then took a long calculated breath whilst he rolled the stem of the glass around, content all eyes were glued on him. That was always James's way, however much he'd perfected the self-deprecation act. When he continued it was deliberately measured yet simultaneously extravagant, master storyteller that he was.

'So as I said, we get to this place and it isn't up to scratch. They've pulled a real fast one on us. From the photos the joint looked top notch. A front deck merging into the white sand of the beach with the crystal-clear Aegean behind. Picture perfect really. The reality was the photo was taken at such an angle it missed out the mud and stone covered road in between, and the dirt bank you had to scramble over to get to the beach. A beach which, might I add, was merely par and not the white sand and crystal-clear water they doctored up on Photoshop.'

He soundtracks his words with a small laugh and, as if it is a stage direction to the expectant faces clustered around him, they all join in enthusiastically. James then relaxes back into the curvature of his seat, visibly happy it's his time now. Safe in the knowledge among this lot, as dinner party host, it was etiquette for him to be allowed to share one good, meaty story. An opportunity he never, ever passed up. Not a care for you, just for his story.

H called it old white man syndrome with a roll of her eye and a sigh. That 'Dad admired the sound of his own voice.'

James would laugh in response, mocking who he was in that oh-so-performed self-deprecation. That's what drew you in in the first place, back when you thought it was sincere. Even though your backgrounds were so wildly different, you had bridged your love through his awareness of who he was and who you were and how apparently none of that mattered in the slightest. And you had adored him for it and so indulged his long-winded stories.

Indulged was probably the wrong word. You had loved them as much as the rest of them, especially on nights like this with the standard local bores James always found room to invite. There were twelve of them in total, dotted along the big teak table centred in the garden of your countryside home. A table hastily dressed up with a white and red tablecloth and sprinkled with good wine and lousy conversation. Clustered under the rustle of the sycamore tree, its angular leaves propelling their way down onto the table as James spoke. The perfect spot for an English summer dinner party like this.

'Naturally we make the best of it, of course we do. B, of course, got stuck right in.'

He'd always called you B, right from the very first day he met you. Never Bella. You often wondered if it was because he didn't like your name, was embarrassed by it even, especially compared to his all-English King name. Your early insecurities had asked if it was too common, too estate. You were christened Bella, not Isabella, after all. The difference mattered. But then your daughter was born and together you chose to name her Helen, yet he called her H from day one and that eased your worries. You soon learned many of his friends did it too. Nickname hungry the lot of them, though not for the people they truly respected.

'We were swimming every day, eating fine Greek cuisine including one joint I can't recommend enough. Worth the air fare alone. A rustic charm to it, yet the food was top notch. Fantastic even.'

To everyone at the table it was another dreamy trip for the picture-perfect family. The happy Halls with their smiling

Christmas cards and summer dinner parties. Only H and you know it was a trip to save your marriage. A second honeymoon of sorts to try and halt the spiral you were on. The fact James would even share a story from such a private, vulnerable moment spoke volumes to the different places you were in.

'In the evening the queue could go on for miles so you'd just put your name down, wander down beach side with a glass of vino to hand, and then wait for your name to be called. I finally finished *Ulysses* whilst waiting to be served at that restaurant, but boy was it worth it. Not *Ulysses* mind, an overlong mess of a novel. Don't understand the hype.'

The guests smiled merrily as James hid one of his own which you knew was blooming underneath his lips. Such a performer, though that was another running thread among his friends. Not necessarily arrogance but an outward facing confidence to thrive in any social surrounding. To always be so comfortable and in control. James was different to his friends on the inside though. Meek at his core, not that anyone really knew. Brightly patterned wallpaper covering the sodden cardboard underneath.

'Anyway, aside from the restaurant we spent the rest of our days zipping around the island on a little moped. Nearly crashed the bloody thing a few times. Uphill on windy roads with B loaded on the back is not what I call smooth sailing.' Again the titters came, not even subtly at your expense.

'A lot of the time though was spent on the beach relaxing with Mr James Joyce, though after the relief of finishing that I soon turned to B's lite-lit which I must say I far preferred.'

You blush when more laughs come because even though it's a compliment of sorts, among this crowd it's most definitely an insult.

'Anyway I digress from the meat of the story. Where crap got real, so to speak.'

A hush descends and James takes a deep, controlled breath, relishing every second that you are hating. You knowing, dreading, what was to come, he craving it.

'So every morning I go out across the mud and stone covered road and scramble down the dirt bank for a morning swim. Nothing like it. Front crawl slicing through the Aegean, not swimming much better than Aegeus with this growing belly, mind you.'

More laughs at a joke that could only work amongst a certain type. James always did know his crowd, equally able to tone it down when he was with your lot. A quality you treasured in him, something you still do. One of the few.

'So this one morning I get up to go out. Quick espresso, a stretch out on the little deck and then I look at to sea. Out to the playground I'm about to dive into. And that's when I see it. Bloody hard to miss.'

'What, James, what?' asks Henrietta longingly. Henrietta with her horse face and English rose dresses who you're eighty percent sure he's having an affair with.

'A boat, a big boat, half wrecked in the bay. Forty-five-degree angle, sort of just hanging there in the bob of the wave. It was one of the most utterly surreal sights that for a moment I couldn't take it in. Just so far removed from our normal mornings you see. After a few beats, once I've gained my sense of self, I wander closer. And that's when I see the people. People everywhere. Some on the boat, some in the water, some diving off the boat into the Aegean. Mainly men, but women and children are there too. And screaming. Couldn't believe it. Quick as a flash I run back to our spot and shake B from her slumber. Now B isn't a morning person, never has been. She can count the sheep

51

until the sun is setting, but this morning she's up in a flash. Responds instantly to what I've seen. Wouldn't expect anything less, social justice, warrior princess as she is.'

You laugh politely and the room smirks along. More compliments wrapped in digs and digs wrapped in compliments, but you'll let him have his moment for now. You've got no choice.

'We both run out to the beach, sprinting towards the boat. I'm kicking sand up in B's face but she doesn't care, only one thing on her mind. When we get there though we realise we have a problem. Well, multiple problems. By now I'd say roughly half of the passengers are onshore, with just the women and children left on board. But also onshore are the Greek police and let's just say they're not like our own bobbies. Ruthless, the lot of them.'

His fawning audience murmurs a nod of approval at this as if they've all come across the Greek police many a time when the reality is you don't get any police out on the private yachts and beaches they frequent. You're the only one at the table who'd think that, mind. They're just a nodding echo chamber and you clench your body tight, trying to resist the urge to share what you need to share.

'So just as we're arriving to help this group of refugees...' He pauses. 'That's who they are by the way, if that part wasn't clear. Refugees the lot of them. Desperate, stranded, alone.'

'Tragic, absolutely tragic,' replies Flora Thompson, who you know for a fact has voted Tory her entire life.

'Just as we're arriving, that's when the police intervene. The beach is just them, the refugees, us, and a few watchers from afar. A true Mexican standoff. Turns out the local Greeks don't get too involved in these matters because the police can come down hard. Easier when you're a tourist and a white one at that. White privilege is what it is, though for once in our life we could use it for some good.'

'Hear, hear,' mutters Ron, a port drinking Reform voter. 'So this policeman, big guy, broad shoulders, far broader than me…' Queue another self-deprecating laugh that conjures up a table of real laughs. '…he throws one palm up in our faces and says, "Go home". Naturally B isn't having any of it, so she carries on towards the group crashed out on the shore. The policeman isn't having any of that though either. Literally grabs her and swings her back to me and repeats, "Go home". Dumbfounded, we're not sure how to respond. Then more police begin to circle and so that's when we retreat. To regroup so to speak.'

'Quite astonishing,' Ron continues, though he looks like he's more focussed on the port than he is on the story. James doesn't care though, he's in full flow, the words rolling off his lips.

'So we go stand under the shade of a barren tree, the sun thrashing down, and try and form a plan. Meanwhile more people are streaming off the boat to shore, whilst some swim back to the boat to help the women and children. I'm all ready to swim out too and lend a hand.'

He lets the self-deprecation act slip for a moment into all out bravado. Nothing is lost however as it only draws admiring, doting stares from Flora and Henrietta.

'But that's when B has a thought. She tells me to wait then quickly scampers off back to the room and I'm left there on my tod just observing it all. This sad boat swaying in the water with the white cliffs towering above. And then I start to think what these poor people must have gone through just to be there. It's a lot to take in.' He takes a long, calculated breath. 'Over time I notice one of them seems to be the ring leader of sorts, communicating with the police and with his fellow refugees. A friendly chap with soft features and a tight beard. Anyway, that's when B returns with a slip of paper in her hand and her mobile

53

phone. It's go time. She immediately starts snapping away, getting everything she can from the shadows where we're somewhat hidden. A right old Marie Colvin in our presence.'

More laughs and you fake a laugh to join them because what else can you do?

'Imagine if you were caught.' Flora lifts from her chair as she says it, her eyes wide.

'Imagine indeed. Luckily of course in that moment we weren't, though I'll come to that later. So after B's got all her snaps, we notice all the police have wandered off to congregate under some shade by the car park. Sensing an opportunity we stealthily make our way across the beach, my toes directing us towards this ring leader. We reach him and I take a glance back at the police and for a few seconds at least, we're in the clear.'

You hear gasps from the table and can only imagine the new smile James is now suppressing. It's the opposite of where you're at. Uncomfortable right down to your stomach for this story even to be told. Doesn't feel like it should be shared, drawing admiration at others' suffering. Suffering that hasn't ended and will only continue with more people just like them. It's similar to how you feel about all those true-crime dramas on the box. James just gobbles them up but you're unable to watch, always thinking about the family on the other end. The ones made to watch a money-making show about how they lost someone dear. And everyone just seems okay with that concept, like everyone is okay now.

' "Hello," I say, walking towards the man, both palms up. My white flag so to speak.' James lifts both hands up in demonstration. ' "We're here to help." The man turns towards me. With poise. Bear in mind we've got no idea if he speaks English at this point, so we all kind of lock in a trance. A few

54

seconds pass and then he replies. "My name is Hassan. We are many. We took a boat from Turkey, though I am from Syria. The drivers of the boats, they left us out at sea and…" He's about to continue but that's when B points out the police are heading our way and at quite a clip. This is where she, my darling B, takes over. She pulls out the piece of paper and hands it straight to this Hassan and says, "This is my number. If you have a phone or can get a phone then send me a message. We want to try and help." Hassan nods, understanding, then scrunches up the paper and shoves it in his pocket just as the police arrive.'

James takes a pause here and reaches for his red. Takes another slow slip and lets the tension of the story wash over his guests. His guests, not yours of course. Like it always has been.

When James and you first got together people kept asking you what you saw in him considering the differences in your background. "Gold digger" others said, but that couldn't have been further from the truth. If anything the family wealth was something that repelled you and took years to get your head around. No, what you saw in James was a great enthusiasm for life. A desire, a need, to truly live life day by day, making the most of each one. A firework constantly burning. Yet over time that waned. Not his raw enthusiasm, that never died. More your appreciation of it. He was just a big kid who never had to take life that seriously and so he didn't. And that started to grate on you as your seriousness began to grate on him.

No doubt from the start there was an element of pride when he married you, of making a point. A wife so different to all his friends who settled for the norm. Here was James, weak old James, marrying 'Jenny from the Block' or whatever it was they used to call you. By now that novelty had worn off though. By now common sense had returned

55

and he had his gaze returned towards his backgrounds' expected type.

'You're holding us on edge here, James, out with it,' yelps Ron, cutting into your thoughts, his red nose growing redder by the second.

James smiles graciously and then continues. 'Apologies, where was I? Oh yes. So the policeman shoves Hassan away. He stumbles a few tragic steps backwards before he falls into the sand. Worried, he then anxiously retreats to his flock, crab-like across the sand. Then the policeman turns to me and grabs the phone in my hand. "You take photos," he screams aggressively in my face as he yanks the phone away. Immediately he goes to my photos and starts looking through, panting under the heat of the Greek sun. A little bead of sweat tunnels down his forehead, a moment of silence reigns and then... he returns me the phone and just says, "Leave. Leave this beach now." Needing no more encouragement we make our exit and dart back to the shadows.'

'But how? What about the photos?' Henrietta squeals, panting almost orgasmically at his words and you're ninety five percent sure they're having an affair.

'What indeed, Hennie,' James replies with a raised brow. 'I deleted them all after taking them. Removed them from my photos, but he didn't check my recycling bin, did he? It was an educated gamble at best, but one that paid off.'

You can't help but snort at his temerity. Temerity. That was a word you'd never heard until you married James. Didn't use that kind of lingo down 'the block', but it's perfect for now. The most outrageous part is no one else notices what he's done. The story clearly starts with you holding the phone and taking the photos, only now James is the one deleting them all into the recycling bin. When this supposed swap happened remains a mystery because it actually is a mystery, especially to you. James's stories always were better when he's front and centre, or at least they are for him. You don't care, it's just the cheek of it, the dismissiveness. You try to catch his eye, but he deliberately avoids it and carries on with his story.

'So what happened next?' barks Ron, taking a short break from his Henry VIII styled gluttony.

'Patience, Ronald, patience. Let a man have a drink.' More laughs as James takes another sip.

'So from the shadows we planned our next move. B was immediately on the internet and searching for who to contact and soon found the digits for a non-profit.' At least he gave you that one. 'I get on the blower and they paint the grim reality. Apparently the Greek police have a habit of sending these boats back out to sea to land on another island that isn't their own. The only way to stop that is public pressure and this is where the safely-stored photos come in. We're promptly carting them across the internet and within a few moments they're slap bang all over Twitter.'

'How wonderful. How utterly wonderful. You hero you.' Hero. Singular.

'I'm so proud of you, James.'

The train steams ahead and you swallow down your rosé with a sigh. Biting your tongue at the depressing irony Flora is in such praise when you saw her recent Facebook posts about boats coming across the Channel.

'I wouldn't say that, Flora. Just doing our bit. Anyone would do the same.'

'Oh, don't be so modest, James,' now Henrietta jumps in and you're now ninety nine per cent sure they're romping in the fields. Got to be happening and you're surprised at how little you care. In fact it's that thought that makes you most sad. This was a man who opened your horizons, who transformed your life, who gave you H and security and a curious love for cricket and Pimms. Yet here you are, barely caring when he tears you down in public before thrusting his tiny penis into Henrietta Wentworth of all people. Life comes at you fast.

'So what happened next?'

Now James pauses as if mulling over her question when you know he's just been counting down the seconds till someone asked. His well-oiled answer polished long in advance of the night.

'We waited. Simply that. Waited to see what would happen. For a few hours we stayed on the beach, unable to leave the boat, scared they might be sent back. There was a little bar on the beach and we'd made friends with a local young Greek chap, so we moseyed on over there to get his two cents. His basic summary, once we'd debriefed everything, was to make ourselves scarce. He was worried about the Greek police now the photos were live and felt we should be too. So after a quick frappé we did exactly that. Got on the moto and jetted off to a different beach to idle away the day. It's hard to get into a book while this is hanging there mind you, so we basically just sat and waited in silence.'

You figure that lie was for Henrietta's benefit because there was nothing silent about that wait. The opposite in fact. It was as if the whole event had briefly charged up your relationship and you were back to being twenty years old again. There was nothing silent about your moans and his grunts as you had the steamiest sex you can remember in a long while. The only silence was after, when you both lay amongst the white sheets of your bed, the curtained door flapping in the breeze, and a raw guilt fell over you both. A shame for finding pleasure that morning when so many others were in such distress. James clearly felt it too, for once on the same page. It was the same guilt that reared its head every time you heard James tell this story, only his was now long gone. 'Then it happened. Ping, the mobile phone went. Ping. I ran to it in a flash as a number I didn't recognise popped up. Hassan was in touch.'

A gasp from Florence, a hand to the horse mouth from Henrietta, an astonished snort from Ron.

'Over the ensuing hours, with Google Translate lending a hand, we slowly got his story. As said, they'd come from Turkey though he was Syrian. Apparently he had two boys in Italy and was heading that way. The boat was on course, then a storm hit and that's how they ended up in Milos. Even before the journey began the vessel was in no fit state, but after the winds started howling it turned into the wreck we witnessed. The charlatans driving the thing gaily jumped ship and all the passengers were left for Mother Nature to decide their fate. Hassan said the ship's captain was a big man, always wearing a pair of bright red sunglasses with a mop of curly brown hair sprouting out above. The whole thing had all been planned in advance, a little escape boat coming to pick up Mr Red Sunglasses and his crew mate before it sunk. Disgusting all round.'

'Astonishing,' Ron remarks, before taking a huge slice of Stilton and clamping it between his jaw. Little crumbled dashes of blue and yellow tumbling like stones off his cleanly shaven chin.

'So what happened next?' Flora now crows, ever the dutiful servant to your husband's ego.

James takes a measured sigh before he continues. 'For the immediate ensuing period, not bloody much. Hassan gave us his location and so we scooted over to a little encampment the police had set up at a neighbouring area.

Conveniently right next to our favourite restaurant, so needless to say we were back in there.'

You cringe but you needn't have bothered. The distastefulness of the action was lost on everyone else.

'Then we just sort of waited around. Tried to read, tried to swim and tried to get to Hassan. Any time we came close though, a policeman would soon appear and bark us away. We did see him once however and shared a solitary wave through the bars of their makeshift prison. After that the holiday was a bit of a damp squib. We took one tour to this darling snorkelling area but instead of enjoying it, we spent the whole time talking to the guide about what had happened. Not the first time he'd seen it. Had a lot of choice words for Mr Red Sunglasses and his ilk. Apparently they do this all the time. Barbarians he called them and I'm inclined to agree. I mean what kind of person could do that? Leaving these innocents, women and children even, out at sea to die. That was a thought which wouldn't leave me. Kept me up at night, stewing over their behaviour. Just not cricket.'

'Well said James,' Florence shouts with a curious force. Again, the Facebook post comes to mind but you're too done with the whole story to even contemplate pointing that out now. 'And so that was all?'

'Not quite.' Now James smiles, his biggest of the night, and your toes can't help but curl at the thought of what is to come.

You can't understand why he does this to himself but these days there's a lot you don't understand. On who your husband has become. Or maybe he was always this way and you were just too lost in the fog of love to see it.

'So we try and help Hassan, do what we can. Got in touch with a few lawyer friends but Hassan isn't keen. Scared of lawyers which makes sense considering. Seems he wants to fly solo on this one and chance his luck to Italy.

60

He still wants the emotional support though and I'm there for him, zipping messages back and forth.'

Again this was obviously you who then relayed everything back to James, but you're too tired to even acknowledge that internally now. Just makes it worse.

'Then one day, the day before we leave, he goes silent. Battery dead. Gone. Finito.'

'Oh my, James, that must have been terrible.' Henrietta exclaims as she plants a hand on his shoulder and gives him a quick rub.

'It was a real shock. We went back to the site a few times but the police presence had grown by now so no chance for any more waving. I just wanted some confirmation you know, something to let on he was okay, but nothing. Again a strange limbo took place and we just prepared ourselves for the end of our trip. We were almost counting down the hours because the whole island felt somewhat eerie now. Disturbing even.'

'I can only imagine. What a remarkable story.'

Your nose scrunches once again at Florence's latest remark and it only tightens when James storms back in. The man you once adored, the man you would do anything for, now this pathetic shell living off your actions and then some. A narcissist of the highest order and you're embarrassed you didn't see it earlier.

'We're not done yet, Flora. No, on the final day there was another twist.'

Here he goes. He's doing it and you almost get up to leave. To stand and walk out of the room because you can't do this. You can't listen to what he's about to say, but if you do leave then this moment will just happen at the next social occasion and the one after that and the one after that and this recurring nightmare is the small thought keeps you in your chair. The chance for a reordering of the truth only you can deliver. One you almost need to deliver for your sense of self, for your sense of being. For you being you and remembering that to the end. And so you take a deep breath, stay glued to your chair and wait.

'On our final day we're milling about in prep for our ferry. It's delayed naturally, typical Greeks, so we've got a few hours to kill. We start rambling our way down the side streets, popping in and out of the shops. B wanders her way into one, eyeing up some ghastly summer dresses. I can't be dealing with that and so I saunter on and take a pew on a bench outside the shop. I'm sitting there, scrolling through the rugby scores, and that's when I see him.'

A collective silence takes hold of the room until Florence breaks it. 'See who, James, see who? Hassan?'

James chuckles to himself, swinging his head from guest to guest. 'Oh no, not Hassan. No, it was Mr Red Sunglasses and curly mop of hair himself. Completely recognisable. Could only be him.'

A gasp takes over the table and it's unbearable. Horrible even, although not for James who is clearly elated. You remember the first time he told you this story. How he broke into the shop you were in with a nervous energy, completely out of breath, to relay to you what had just happened. His eyes almost glazed over, intoxicated. The words spewing out in an uncontrollable barrage.

'For a moment I was speechless. I just couldn't believe it. My heart began to pound in its cage, the drums of the Vikings roaring against my ribs. Then I realised it was time to act. I had to; there was no other way. I rose from my bench slowly and started walking towards him. It was just the two of us down this side alley, a little corridor of beauty I might add. Cobbled stones beneath my feet, little blue shuttered windows around me. Zeus no doubt smiling down from above. Then I made my move.'

"You sir, you." Slowly, very slowly, he turned to face

me. "What do you want?" Now my courage bloomed and I stood tall. "I know you, I said. I know what you've done. A smuggler. Leaving those poor people to die.'"

'Well you should have seen the expression that took over his face. Pure bewilderment for a dash, before composure returned. "I don't know what you're talking about," his voice deep and low, the croak of a man who's smoked a million ciggies. "Oh but you do, señor.'"

'And that's when he knew. He knew that I knew and he knew I was about to kick up a fuss. And that's precisely when we moved from the frying pan into the fire, so to speak. Quickly I reached for my phone, though in hindsight I maybe should have done that from the start. Emotion had got the better of me.'

The grip James now had on the room was impressive. Awe, shock and wonder on all their faces.

'Seeing the phone he starts to panic and so makes a go at me. Dives forward for the phone, but luckily I'm ready for him. Light on my feet I skip to the side and that's when my years of playing ruggers comes into play. I drop low and hit him with a tackle from the side. Right into his shins my shoulder gets him and down the Jenga pieces fall. Then it's man to man on the floor and an all-out scramble begins.'

Fingers are over your eyes now, unable to watch, unable to listen. Just like H used to when you would embarrass her. H who, if it wasn't for her existence, you'd be furious at all those years wasted on such a pathetic individual. A daughter who made a marriage worthwhile. Yet she's long gone now, living her life in London. All loved up with her eyes on kids, whilst you're at the other end of the ladder. And it's that thought, knowing how far away she is, knowing she's never coming back that makes the loneliness so much worse, and propels you finally to act.

63

'He's holding me down, then me him. Back and forth, a dance of titans.' All self-deprecation now lost long ago.

'For a moment I think I've got him. I really do, pinned down and merciless below me. But alas I had eyes bigger than my stomach and I did not notice the knife he slid out from his lower trouser pocket. In a flash it was to my neck and the struggle immediately ceased and we're just two bodies panting on the cobblestone floor.'

More gasps, more astonishment, Henrietta's fingers dancing down the nape of his neck.

'Slowly I raise both hands up in peace, put them behind my head and lift from the position I was in on top of him. Mr Red Sunglasses laughs at me, laughs loudly, as if he's won. No awareness or humility of the cheating techniques that led him there. I stand and change my gears into reverse. One step, two. Then he stands to meet me, before backing off down the street behind. Still facing me mind you, the knife pointed at my chest. Once he's ten or so paces away he turns and bolts, running his way down alleys and I'm left panting alone in the street.'

'My God, James, old boy,' Ron proclaims, his attention for once with the story. 'Very well played indeed. Didn't know you had it in you.'

And that's probably the truest thing said at the table all night. Because James doesn't have it in him. Even when you loved him beyond belief, he never had it in him. He was always a coward. Proud to call you his wife but uncomfortable to walk the roads you once called home. Squirming his way down them, clinging to you for comfort. The story truly is unbelievable because it literally is, but none of the others see it.

'Oh, James, how brave of you. How very, very brave.' Henrietta moves closer to him then remembers where she is, darts you a guilty glance and falls back into her seat.

Saving her kisses for later or tomorrow or the next work trip or whenever it is they meet.

'Just doing what needed to be done. Couldn't do otherwise.'

And this is your moment. You can't take it anymore, it's all too nauseating. This is your chance to give James the justice he deserves. For all the humiliations thrown your way, not just this night but to all those others too. The put downs, the dismissiveness of any career, all the things he once rallied against when you were young to which he is now guilty. And not just to you but also to the poor people on the boat and their unwanted role as an ego pumper for this man they've never met. And for H and all the stories she has had to endure despite the distance he's always shown her as a parent. This and that and that and this and Christ you could go on. Yes, this is your moment to strike. To say the truth out loud, but for some reason you can't. You can't bring yourself to say it loud. Maybe because you know the weight of the room is against you, or maybe because you're still scared of what it will mean. You start to sweat, the moment fading in front of your fingertips, knowing you may never get it again.

Yet it's in that moment when James catches your eye.

It's a quick look, a sly one, but how grateful you are he did. It finally gives you the opportunity and your strength roars into life, remembering the person you are, the person you sort of forgot. When your eyes meet you look at him, stare deep down into his small, timid soul and you raise your eyebrows high and you laugh.

A quiet laugh but a laugh all the same. For a second he looks confused and then slowly it dawns on him. Dawns on him that you know, and even if you don't let everyone else know, he now knows you know. Like you did the last time he told this story and the time before that, but this time at

65

least you're letting him know, and oh how he does. You see his pupils shrink, the sweat on his brow, his fingers now playing anxiously with each other whilst his right ear starts to twitch, something H always did when she was nervous. And in that moment you finally feel content, like some justice has been delivered.

Because you know the truth about that day he ran into the shop to find you looking at Greek literature, not ghastly sundresses and he told you his story in panting breath. About the man in the red sunglasses and the fight and the knife. He now knows you saw exactly what happened, even though you've never told him. Endured it till now, at first because you were so shocked by what he was saying that you couldn't quite believe it, and then because you almost couldn't say it out loud because the second you did you knew it would shatter your whole relationship. And even though you needed to, some things are easier said than done. His whole facade of masculinity would be destroyed in a moment and knowing James, knowing the true man he was, there would be no moving forward.

But now you've heard this story too many times and so finally, with a small look, you've let him know when you were in that shop reading a blurb on a book about Plato, through the window the same man in red sunglasses caught your eye too. Completely recognisable as James had said, that part was true. And then you watched as James clocked him. Watched as you saw your husband's face calculate what to do. And watched and watched as James withered back into his seat like a delicate little petal in a winter's storm, his right ear twitching. And that's all that happened. That was literally it. No confrontation, no rugby tackle, no fight, no knife, no bolt down the alleyways, even no thought to call the police. Instead, you watched James, sat on the bench, panting uncomfortably in the shade. For five minutes he sat there, the man in red sunglasses long gone. Then he stood up, brushed himself down and ran to find you in the shop to tell you his story. And that was that. That was James's way.

Part of your heart bled when he told you. A realisation this is what James wished he had done, what he hoped of himself. What he would and should have done, and so he built up a tale instead. To imagine the man he could be and then maybe believed he was, as he told it to anyone and everyone. Gone was the self-deprecation and instead it was a complete self-mutilation and it was horrifying to watch. But by now it had gone too far and that's why you gave the look and with that the walls of your marriage would crash down. But you can accept that now and can even admire the way you did it. Not publicly, not brazen nor aggressive but in a subtle, cutting way. Just like James taught you.

Dear Babbo

Dear Babbo,

I am sad for not writing sooner. Things have been a little tough at the shop with far lower sales than predicted. We'll turn it around, we always do, so don't worry. I just keep wondering what you would do? Though even as I write that, I know you'd never have got us in this position in the first place.

The competition is just so fierce now, so many new businesses within the city walls. Our work is still wonderful but is there the appetite for such high quality, expensive suits anymore, especially with the economy as it is? Not to mention all the cheap imitators on the market, selling suits for half the price. No doubt half the working conditions for their makers too, but the buyers choose to ignore that even when they cry green. Oh, the hypocrisy of today. It's not hard to imagine you ranting about it too if you were here.

Anyway, I will write something longer soon with some real, shop-unrelated news.

Tutto il mio amore,
Gio

12th May

Dear Babbo,

News at last. I am sorry for taking so long since the last letter, this one will be more thorough as promised. You know how it gets with the shop. You'll be happy to know that things have been better this last month – it's a relief to have wedding season here. We had clients from Rome, Naples, and a lot from

Florence. Some Lucchesi but that's been less recently, I think due to the economy.

I guess there are some positives as we even had some Inglese in the shop this week. Very rare these days. Friendly people who brought those famous Inglese habits with them. They are in town for a week, visiting family friends who had recently moved to one of the towns outside of the city. I will tell you about them as I can just picture you and Mamma smiling when you read this. It will also be nice to write about something that isn't the state of the shop for once, even though I know it's what you want.

So they came to the shop on the Tuesday at around twelve. The husband, the wife, and the six-months-old baby. For an hour the husband tried on suits while the wife nursed their baby in the corner of the shop. He was a sweet bambino with long curling eyelashes. Irene was besotted with him as I'm sure you can picture. Anyway, after multiple tries to find the right suit, we settled on a classic. One of yours. A deep blue linen jacket matched with some white, slim fit trousers. He wanted blue trousers, but I convinced him into white. An Italian style for an Inglese. I even added the cream white pocket handkerchief for a final touch, folded in such a way to create two triangles peeking out from the rim of the pocket. Just as you taught me. In that moment I was reminded of what you always said, the quote you stole from your great hero:

'To create something exceptional your mindset must be relentlessly focussed on the smallest detail.'

The line you used to say to me again and again and I finally think I am living it true. That I have learned.

69

Of course the husband loved these added touches and the suit in general, and so did the wife. I think she was even happier than him. He was scruffy when he walked in, a true traveller type despite his age, yet now he was transformed. Even I couldn't imagine the impact the suit would have on him.

Radiant is the only word I can think of and it reminded me why we do this work. Why you worked so hard to build this business from the ground up when everyone told you no. The endless power of beauty and what that can do to people. How even the brutish Inglese can be overwhelmed in joy by what we create. It really is testament to your legacy. Anyway, I'm off topic. My hand is tired from the day's work, so these letters take me longer than they should.

As said, the couple were happy with the suit; it just needed a few tweaks to get the length of the leg perfect. Three fingers from the floor of course, the only way. It's sad how I was so nervous when I used to say that. I'd watched you do it so many times yet it never felt my advice to give. It felt so you and for so long I never felt like I'd earned the right to say it myself, however much you encouraged me. I think that's why so many people, especially Lucchesi, questioned me at the start. They could sense my nervousness. I'm almost embarrassed to look back at the suit seller I once was. How different to now.

They tell stories of me in the streets these days. I've even overheard some myself when they don't know it's me listening. 'The flamboyant, eccentric Roberti with the Principe Azzurro hair. You must go see his shop, even if just to meet him.' Probably a homosexual they say, even though everyone in the city walls knows Lili and the bambini. Italians love to gossip; I can't moan about that. In truth I think it helps sales in the shop instead of damages them. How different from what they used to say.

'The boy living off his Babbo's hard work. Desperate to learn the craft but no skill, no confidence...'

Ah, I go off topic again. It must be the wine talking. Lili is already asleep and the bambini too. I probably should join them, but it's so hard to go from the adrenaline of the shop straight to bed. I know you felt the same. One needs this time to decompress and writing to you helps me do that. I just apologise for how long it's taken and now the rambles of this letter, though I guess you're used to them by now. Part of the charm, I hope.

So, after sending the suit off to be tailored we agreed upon a time for them to return to collect it. The only one available was at seven the next day, not long before we closed. I told him I couldn't wait to see him and even gave them a discount, though I made it look far greater than it was. Again, just as you taught me. After that I gave him my card and my personal number. Yes, this is something new that I am doing.

See next week they are off to a wedding at St. Paul's Cathedral – a true favourite of yours. I always loved it too. Imagine this though, the couple were not looking forward to the wedding even though it is for the woman's father! One of the great buildings of all time for her babbo's wedding, yet they're unsure whether to go. Apparently it is his second marriage, 'an affair' the daughter said, and she stood on the side of her Mamma which makes sense, but still... St Pauls! They must come from a certain family line however as not any old individual can get married there.

Do you remember when we visited it together, one of our last trips? For an hour we just stood there and looked at it, taking it all in. Christopher Wren, though I know you know that. He may not possess the attention to beauty as some of ours do, but he was so prolific. That man designed and built over fifty churches after the Great Fire of London. A fire that destroyed a city and yet out of it came such art. Such greatness rising from the ashes. I've always found that so powerful. So poetic.

Now back to this wedding at St. Paul's. See this is one of the great changes from when you were in charge: social media and the internet. Now businesses cannot survive without it. I am still an amateur but I try to adapt and this man gave me a chance. I asked him to take a photo at this wedding next week in front of St. Paul's wearing our suit. He will then put it on his social media and do something called a 'tag' of our page. The knock-on effect of this social media post is that it will hopefully bring more people to us and our work. How times have changed, yet now it's the most effective way to sell. No longer can we rely on simple word of mouth... Sorry Babbo, I promised to not talk about the shop and yet here I am. Like father like son, as the locals say. I will try again.

Back to the Inglese, we agreed upon seven the next evening and the husband was good to his word. He arrived at exactly the right time, very Inglese of him, though this time he was alone.

'Where are your wife and child?'

The man did not think much of the question and just replied, 'Back at the hotel.'

'But why not bring them with you?' I probed with more urgency or 'flamboyancy' as they say.

72

I could tell Irene was disappointed not to see the little baby again as I know she wants one of her own soon. What Italian woman doesn't? I hope she finds the love she deserves.

'My wife must be in the hotel room while the baby sleeps,' the Inglese continued.

'Sleeps?' I questioned. 'It's only seven.'

Then the man looked straight at me, his expression one of utter confusion.

'Exactly,' he said, his tone firm. 'The baby went down nearly one hour ago.'

'Is he ill?' Irene now interjected, concern on her face.

'Ill? Not at all,' the Inglese laughed. 'That's just his bedtime. He goes to bed at six every night. He's on a good schedule, so H, my wife, is staying in the hotel room with him. Can't mess with the schedule or we'll have hell to pay.'

Six! Can you imagine! You should have seen the look on Irene's face. Astonishment, outrage and more. Babies going to bed at six in the evening. In Italy! I've never heard of such a thing. After the man left Irene was still in shock.

'Brutta, brutta,' she kept saying on repeat. The Inglese are so funny. Always different to the rest, like it's a badge of pride they like to wear.

Finally I got there, the end of my long story. I hope it provides you some smiles when it reaches you. Please share it with Mamma too. I miss you both more than you can imagine. How I wish you were here with me to help sail through these windy seas we face. I know you'd adapt to the social media thing far better than any of the other old tailors in town. That's what always stood you out from the rest. That ability to adapt.

On that note, I will leave you both, but another letter will follow soon. Hopefully with even better news and stories.

Tutto il mio amore,
Gio

8th July

Dear Babbo,

Again, a long time has passed. I'm so sorry. The bambini are growing fast and although they don't know it, they miss your presence very much. I can sense it. A hole in their life without the regular contact with their nonno and nonna. That is life and there's nothing much we can do about it, but I miss you too. My heart aches daily, especially when the shop struggles. I feel I damage the family name, even when I give it my all. Who'd have thought that when I was a young boy travelling the world, walking out on the family against all your asking otherwise, I'd now miss you so much? Not only that, but how I might bring more shame to the family name now than I did back then.

It's sad to think of all the arguments we had. We were both different people who then mellowed with age – wouldn't you say? Mistakes were made by us both, although I still stand by what I did. I wouldn't be the person I am today if I did not make my leave. I wouldn't value family, kindness and compassion like I do now. I needed those travels, even if they hurt both you and Mamma. Your lack of support wounded me also.

I love Italy and loved Italy back then but I also needed a break from it, from the city walls. Now I value how close families are here. I still see so many

74

friends living near their relatives and it's a wonderful thing. Something I did not understand when I was young. But also there is space for exploring and finding out things about yourself away from the family nucleus and I needed to do that. I found it so hard you couldn't empathise with those thoughts.

I always remember the realisation that hit when we watched the motorcycle travel film about Che Guevara together. It was like a rocket shot through me and all I wanted to do was travel to Latin America and uncover more about the world. Your instant response was a negative one, siding with the communist miners in the film and their surprise people travel to just travel.

'What a luxury you said, a rich man's fantasy,' as if you were the same as them and not a business owner selling high-end suits to the rich, holidaying in Puglia and Venice. It was a hypocrisy I couldn't bear and, all combined, it eventually led me to leave.

I would never take back that decision even though I know what hurt it caused. Now I can see how clearly it helped me follow in your footsteps, just as you dreamed. Without that trip it would have been impossible. Like a man who sleeps around before he settles down and marries, I had an itch I needed to scratch and scratch it I did. I never got to tell you about those trips and that was your fault. Your old man stubbornness. You were a wonderful babbo but also had such a simple, narrow view of life and I feel sad that you never got to experience some of the things I did, or at least experience them through me. You could never allow yourself and subjected Mamma to the same rules, even when she desired more.

Maybe that's why you were so successful in the

shop whilst I struggle? You were so determined to succeed, so focussed on one thing and I lack that, though is that a bad thing? I don't want to be in the shop until ten at night and not say goodnight to the children. Did you once make that sacrifice? Sacrifice. I laugh only because the existence of that word in your vocabulary, in your everyday defence of your actions, should never have existed. I choose my family and would do every time though I do wish the shop would flourish, too. Maybe those two things cannot exist together like you used to allude. That you must choose one. I will work my best to challenge that narrative. To be a good babbo and a good business owner at the same time. Let's see which one of us is right. Does Italy allow a true, modern, feminist man? I am not sure.

I also fear things may only get harder with what's happening next door. There's been movement for months in Signora Andrea's old shop. I feared what it might be and yesterday had it confirmed. A new suit shop. A chain that runs through Rome, Florence, Naples and even Milan. Let's just hope the quality is like some of those other chain stores. It's that and only that which helps us survive. I'll keep you posted.

Tutto il mio amore,
Gio

24th July
Dear Babbo,
All our worries have come to life. Not only is the new chain store next door a far cheaper alternative than what we offer, the quality is surprisingly good. I went by earlier this morning and have rushed back to

send this. The linen jackets are so fine and light yet also inexpensive, which makes me wonder how? The answer lies in Asia, of course. I thought the changing world and so-called commitment to a green future could help us but it feels like that hasn't hit Italy yet. Late as ever.

At least we have Irene who is still far better than any other seller in town. You trained her well. Together, I still think we have a fighting chance. As you often used to say, where there is life there is hope. The thought of you barking that loud as you stomped around the house still brings me great comfort. More news coming soon.

Tutto il mio amore,
Gio

3rd October

Dear Babbo,

So long since last I wrote you. As I'm sure you have already guessed, it's because of the shop. We've been doing longer and longer shifts late into the night, throwing everything we can to turn things around. I won't lie, it's been hard, and it terrifies me.

Irene had to ask for a week off as she's so exhausted, so this week I worked alone. Lili brings the kids into the shop to spend time with me there because I am returning home later and later (though luckily they don't get to bed as early as un bambino Inglese!). I still refuse to make the same choices you made but now perhaps understand you better now.

Meanwhile, next door the customers stream in even though the summer season is over. On a site called Instagram – one of these social media things I told you about – they have over 700 thousand followers. We have 452.

So many staff, so many resources behind them. It's like Juventus against Atalanta. Let's just hope their Juventus gets caught in some financial difficulties or cheating again, otherwise I worry we are done.

As for the bambini, they're growing fast. Matteo is nearly one now and Monica is three. They both smile a lot though Matteo is growing more stubborn, just like his nonno.

Within the city walls life remains the same though a new restaurant has opened near the shop. We went last week and although the food was fine it lacked the same kind of attention and care as some of the older restaurants. On the surface the place appeared stylish and fresh but the food felt rushed, a crust undercooked, a sauce overcooked. Almost symbolic of everything inside the walls these days. It just means I go back to the established places outside where the care remains. Let's just hope those favourite spots don't become too popular and fall to the same kind of failings as a result.

That's all for now, back to work.

Tutto il mio amore,
Gio

26th December

Dear Babbo,

Buon Natale!

Where has this year gone? I guess the answer to that lies in the shop. To say we are struggling is not a classic dramatisation for our family, it's sadly the truth.

Irene and I are in there day and night and it's not

nearly enough. The shop next door is killing us and they seem proud to do so. Two weeks ago the manager came by the store with a card for Natale. He was polite and friendly and asking us how we are doing, but I saw laughs behind every question.

When I said things were bad, he just said, I did wonder why it was so cold in here.

And then he took that as his time to go.

Can you believe it? Businesses in Italy used to support each other, used to look after each other, even under the dark days of Mussolini. Now no more. They want to see us fail and failing is exactly what we're doing. I am sorry, Babbo, to oversee this descent down to the underworld, but I have not given up hope yet. We keep fighting, as shown by our latest sad news to share… we sold the family home.

Again, I'm sorry, but it was getting to the stage I was having to think about letting Irene go. I saw no other way financially, even though alone it would be impossible. However, instead of losing her, Lili and I made another decision. We just couldn't face letting her go, not only as a worker but also as a dear friend. She is too important to us and so material things must go first and the only real financial alternative was to leave our place within the city walls.

I know how important that home was to you, yet I also know the shop is more so and this was the only way to keep Irene. The house sold for more than expected, the city is such a growing tourism destination these days, so that was a welcome boost. We've now moved outside of the city to one of the picturesque little towns, a fifteen minute drive away. It's so peaceful out here and maybe I even prefer it. There is lots of nature around us and the bambini have room to play outdoors.

It's so much cooler, too, I never realised. The house itself is small, but part of an old farm. Nothing grows there but I have dreams of starting it again. We could make our own oil, wine, grow fruit and vegetables. It shouldn't be too hard to set up, I just need time. Time I sadly don't have right now.

Living around us are lots of Italians, families that have lived here for a long time and they welcome us like one of their own. Some even know of you. 'The famous Roberti', they say and they tell me stories of your life in the shop but also before that, when you were a young man causing mischief. A young man who never worked they said, partying and eating and sleeping his way across the city. Stories I never knew but wish I did. In honesty, I'm sad you never shared them with me or showed compassion and understanding when I was that same young man. Instead you put water on my youth and tried to tie me down. It's upsetting to think of all the good times we could have had and I only know that because of these new neighbours I've only just met.

It's not just the old families who live around us though. The area is growing more diverse by the day. This new wave of immigration has hit Toscana too and somehow, some have ended up in our town. Not many, but a few. There is one man here called Hassan who lives with his two sons. When he is settled and has enough money he hopes to bring his wife and daughter here. You should hear the stories of this man, Babbo, the things he has been through just to be here, to be alive.

It's made me realise that however bad things get with the shop, I also need perspective. We have a house, a business, a beautiful family and I must remember that, even when I despair. This man helps me grasp that,

80

though I worry about Lili. Her previously restrained anxiety can be resisted no longer. Even though she tries her best to hide it, she never can. At night she has stopped sleeping. At four she will be up, busy in the kitchen, unable to sleep, unable to sit still. Remaining busy because what else can she do?

To help with money she has picked up some cleaning work for one of the nearby houses. A website called Airbnb that's everywhere now. People renting out their houses at the weekend and charging a fortune to Americans for them. Americans who have a great, great, great, grandfather that was Italian and now they're searching out their bloodline for any hint of Italian, proud to discover it.

If only your uncle was around to hear that after all his troubled years in America where he did his best to hide his roots. What was the name he chose again? Charlie? The Italian Charlie! I laugh just writing it. Changing his name so no one knew, even though it was obvious. Now they do the opposite and want everyone to know, all naming their children something Italian. I saw Luca is the thirtieth most popular baby name in America now. Society changes fast. Regardless, the work helps her, keeps her busy, but the money isn't enough.

If only you were closer to help. We need it now more than ever. I keep telling myself it will get better, that it will change. I just need the perspective my new neighbour's life gives me. Though at night, with a glass in my hand, I can't help but think what life was like before this shop next door arrived. How it was so much easier when it was Signora Andrea's little place. How life would be so much better if this shop was gone, vanished. Based on the customers I see leaving,

81

a suit in their hand, I can't see that happening any time soon. I can dream though. I can always dream.

Tutto il mio amore,
Gio

Dear Babbo,

A short letter as nothing positive to share. Barely any sales, low season lower than ever before. Not sure how much longer we can last but Irene and I are trying. We even messaged the Inglese for the St Paul's photo and guess what? Turns out they never even went to the wedding. The dad apologised but said at the last minute his wife decided she couldn't go.

"Too political" were his words. That it was a family matter and they went to the pub with her betrayed mum instead. Sums up our luck right now. I'll write a longer letter soon.

Tutto il mio amore,
Gio

28th March

Dear Babbo,

This is the letter I never wanted to send. It's hard for me even to write this but there was no other way – I had to let Irene go. We just didn't have enough to pay her. Even with Lili's job and selling the house, it still wasn't enough. There was nothing I could do.

I think she knew it was coming but it didn't make it any easier. I told her slowly, holding both her hands, promising her a job when things got better. At the start she took it well and her expression never changed. She just listened and nodded and told me *she understood. I was relieved, expecting worse. Then a customer walked in but she couldn't bring herself to face them. Instead she darted out back and while I tried to sell a suit – and failed because the price was apparently too high – I could hear her cries. Sobbing at first and then louder and louder.*

Luckily the customer left quickly and so I rushed to find her curled in a ball on the floor, her body shaking uncontrollably. I didn't know what to do, Babbo. I've never felt so awful and so alone. Did you ever have to let anyone go? I doubt it, after all you were the one who hired Irene all those years ago. All I could do was get on the floor next to her. I wrapped my arm around her and held her tight and told her it would be all right, but I knew that wasn't true. And in that moment it hit me too. And so while she cried, I cried. Not as loud, but just as hard. A wreck, both of us. I just hoped a customer didn't walk in then and hear us, but guess who soon did... next door's manager.

It's like he knew the news before I even delivered it. He knows quality when he sees it, I've seen him watching Irene from the window. Anyway once Irene and I had tidied ourselves up and gone onto the shop floor, he was there waiting. Offered her a job on the spot. Imagine my feelings. Anger and relief at the same time. She didn't know what to do, what to say. Just looked at me, her eyes needing an answer as she couldn't say yes on her own. And what could I say?

The reality is we would need something spectacular to hire her again. That's the truth, but I couldn't say it in front of this man. So I told him to leave, tongue-lashed him out of the shop. Not very professional but I'm broken. Then, when he was gone, I gave Irene my blessing. I had to. I'm truly pleased this opportunity came, even if it breaks me. It means we can stay close, that she and Lili can remain friends. And that was that, we were done.

The next day I went to work and just as I was arriving I saw Irene enter their shop, nervously making her way in and it killed me. I had to turn away, concentrate on opening the shutters, unlocking the doors and then went to work in silence. Complete silence. I put music on just to stop the thoughts in my head getting too loud. The anger and the hatred. It's like all my failings I now blame on this shop next door because I don't know where else to direct them. Where else can they go? Towards Italy? Towards me? Towards you? Every night is the same, I'm as awake as Lili now. Working, drinking, despair. I'm not sure how much longer I can last.

Tutto il mio amore,
Gio

3rd May
Dear Babbo,
I dream every night you are well and happy. That you and Mamma are laughing and drinking and eating good food. That the air is warm and the company you keep is pleasant. Sometimes I wish I could be there too and maybe that day isn't so far away. Every day here is worse. People barely enter the shop anymore and I understand why. It's a mess compared to what it used to be. Everything is on sale now which means we sell, but the margin is so small it's pointless. At least the few customers we have are happy.

I can barely sleep anymore unless I drink enough, and then I just wake up tired, grumpy and irrational.

I think Lili might leave me soon. I can sense she has had enough and I can't blame her. I'm not the person I was or want to be, but I can't change it either. I'm so lost, more lost than I've ever been. Where has the fun-loving traveller gone? The happy husband and father? The flamboyant suit seller? All memories now.

Gio

23rd June

Dear Babbo,

No good news, so no reason to write. The money has stopped completely. Lili and I just argue now, no love left. Neither of us have the energy. The kids can feel it too, they're older now, more aware, especially Monica. I barely see them even though when I'm in the shop I barely work. Just sit and stare. Sometimes I close up and go to the bench in front and sit and watch the people stream into next door. Irene is in there every day, she looks happy at least. Once she saw me and waved though I couldn't bring myself to wave back. I need it all to change but I don't know how.

Where are you to help?

Gio

28th August

Dear Babbo,

Sad days, dark days, laughter all gone. The only thing that now brings me joy are the smiles of the bambini and the food and wine of the countryside. Everything else brings darkness, even the suits. Now when I look at them I just see what they've done to

85

me, to us, to my family. The pain they have caused and for what? The famous Roberti name? I want to give it all up, I need to give it all up, but I can't. And you know the reason why? You Babbo, you. Always you. Pressuring me, asking more of me, demanding more of me, even from where you are now.

Gio

14th November

Babbo,

Lili has left me. She had to. We couldn't go on any longer, neither of us had anything left to give. It was unfair on the bambini, unfair on her. They've stayed in the house and I sleep in the shop now. It's like a prison I can never leave. At night I bring the shutters down and sit in darkness, waiting for morning to come. I can't remember the last time I slept a night through. The only time I leave is to bring these letters to you.

Gio

25th December

Babbo,

Buon Natale.

I'm sorry. Sorry for the son I was, for the failure I have brought to this shop, to our family, to our name. The shop is no more, I don't even open it for customers. There's no point, the bills are too high. I've spoken to next door and the manager is interested in buying it as he naturally wants to expand. I think I am going to say yes.

My friend Hassan, the man I told you about, has said I can stay with him and I write this from his home now

86

surrounded by his precious family. I am near the bambini and that brings me joy, even if nothing else does. Lili does not want them to know about our separation yet and refuses the idea of divorce, purely on how it would look within the community. Emotionally however we are divorced and I feel empty inside as a result. Broken. A hollowed-out carcass in comparison to the individual I once was.

What sad news to share on this special day – one I celebrate with a family who only do so out of a kindness to me and all I've been through. I'm not sure where I would be without them. Such a show of generosity from foreigners whilst I am deserted by my own. It's hard to know what to make of it.

Anyway, that is all for now. Buon Natale, I hope your day is brighter than mine.

Gio

2nd January

Babbo,

The sale has happened, the shop is Roberti no longer. I hand over the keys in just over a week. Finally I feel some sort of relief but that is always masked by what you must now feel. Well, that is my problem no more. I am a free man now.

Gio

12th February

Oh Babbo. A new year brings new news. Dark, sad news. What I write now is perhaps the most difficult letter I've ever had to write but also who are we as humans if we don't face up to our mistakes and where

87

we have gone wrong? And face up to them I have, with everyone but you. The hardest person I must tell.

There is no simple way to say it, so here it is: the shop is no more, it's is gone, forever. The Roberti stronghold vanished from history and not in the way you must think. I am glad I cannot see your face when you read this, but I know I must write it. To tell you the truth.

The thing is I lost everything. Everything and everything they stole from me with their cheap suits and busy shop and expansions. The shop, Irene, the house, Lilli and the bambini. They took them all and so I did something back. An eye for an eye as the Bible says. Was I wrong? Maybe, but life is not always possible to live in the glow of hindsight and so I did what I did and that is the end of it. At least I can write with clarity of mind now, something I lost these last few months, and with that clarity I only ask that you can forgive me ...

It was my last night in the shop, the night before they took it for good. I wanted to sleep in the shop that night, not at Hassan's even though I have been staying there a lot. That last night I wanted to be close to you for one final time, to our legacy. Do you understand that? So I locked up early, closed the doors and breathed it all in. The suits were still there as I had agreed to sell them all to next door too, at a discount of course. So it was just me and all our handiwork, our ideas and designs. Surrounded by beauty, by our craftsmanship, our history. I soaked it all in for the last time, drinking more and more as the night went on. In many ways it was the perfect end.

At one point, maybe three in the morning, I decided to venture outside as I needed the fresh air.

It was a cold night, quiet in the streets. I stumbled out, drink in my hand and out of nowhere tripped, lurching forward until I crashed to the floor. Down in the cold on the cities' cobbled streets. A sad sight, Gio Roberti fallen so low. And then from my broken position, a wretch of the streets sprawled across the floor, I looked up and there it was before me. Laughing at me like it has ever since it arrived. The shop next door, silently taunting me.

And in that look, in that hate fuelled glance, an idea came and I did not have the composure to say no. My mind floated back to the Inglese I told you about and to St. Paul's and Christopher Wren. Of how beauty rose from the ashes and how that could happen again. And once the thought was there it just took over and there was no other way.

I rushed back in the shop and got to work. Did you know linen was so flammable? I found out once at a wedding. A cigarette to my arm, a suit ruined. The memory had stayed with me and so in the shop I got out the scissors, the same, blue-handled pair you had when you were a boy, and began to cut. Tearing suits off their hangers and slicing into the beautiful fabric. In a craze I worked, chopping, chopping, chopping. Then I picked up all the rags and began shoving them into two half-drunk bottles that littered the shop floor.

Alcohol you would be ashamed of. No fine wines anymore, just potions made to help you forget. You know them of course, but only because we used them once to make limoncello. You and I in the shade of the garden on a warm summer's eve, picking our lemons while Mamma smiled on. Pouring that toxic liquid over those ripe Sicilian lemons to make our special drink.

And now I used that same alcohol to burn. A Molotov cocktail they call it, originally from Finland, from the war. I walked outside with two, one in each hand, then stood to face the shop next door. I almost wish someone had seen me. Two arms raised like Christ on the cross. A flaming bottle in each, Cattedrale di San Martino behind me. One breath, two, and then I threw them. Threw them both with all I had and watched as they crashed through the shop window. Watched as next door's cheap suits took the flames. It wasn't long though before the fire roared, eating everything inside. Flames licking every part of the shop and I let out a strange guttural scream of delight. I had done what needed to be done. Justice for everything they'd done to me. Or so I thought. In the end, who am I to give out justice? Just a man whom the world owes nothing. Justice is not for me to decide.

See, as the flames roared they roared too high and when the fire grew it took our dear, little shop too. Took it all in a second. I ran inside to try and save it. Ran to get the fire extinguisher buried under the counter, but what can a fire extinguisher do against fire like that? And what can a man do? The fire took me too, burning up my arms, smoke consuming my lungs. I sprayed the extinguisher wildly in all directions as I tried to make my exit, but I was nothing compared to what surrounded me. The flaming haunted suits silently mocking me.

Then I crashed back out onto the street, no longer cold but ablaze in heat like a summer's day. And there I passed out thinking of you and of Mamma and of all I've done wrong.

The police took me first thing, though it's not like

I tried to fight it. I was there and waiting in my half-burned suit, my arms raw, my eyes stinging. Irene saw it all happen, tears streaming again as I got put inside a car. Another job I've stolen from her. Driven away to where I have been for the last month now, sat in my cell in a thin piece of cotton, cheap and ill-fitting. No more suits for me. Lili refuses to visit me so I'm not sure when I will see the bambini again.

All I have now are these letters to you, letters that will never get returned. The guards said I need an actual address for this letter to be sent to you, and they won't hand deliver it to your grave. That it's not possible and they mocked me for even making the suggestion.

Truthfully I feel relief if you don't read this. I'm not sure I could deal with you and Mamma learning of what I've done from wherever you now are. In writing it I have tried though and in the shop I tried, too. In my marriage, with Matteo and Monica. Just sometimes trying is not enough. That is life's sad reality.

I hope one day you can find forgiveness for me like I have for you. Because you are part of this, it's just taken me a lifetime to realise that. See you made the cocktail with me. I'm just the man who sparked the match.

Tutto il mio amore,
Gio

The Haunted Priest

Rolando Vargas's dad was murdered on September 26th, 1967. He was shot, cold blooded, in the hills just north of La Higuera, by a CIA-trained member of the Bolivian military.

Rolando was just nine at the time, a bullet to his heart too, and all because of, in his words, 'the stupidity of two naive visionaries.' One was his father, Alvaro Vargas. The other was Argentinian-born revolutionary and Cuban icon, Ernesto Che Guevara.

I only know all this because Rolando told me, hunched over an old wooden table out the back of the Catholic church where he worked. His voice soft like the crunch of snow underfoot, papaya seeds caught between crevices of his last teeth. A mouth stained a light orange hue due to years of chewing coca leaves. A habit unusual for a modern priest yet one he did with no fear of ignominy.

As for me, I was a young travel writer looking to make a name for myself, listening to this forlorn, haunted priest, sharing his story for the first time. Laying out his life to me over one long, confusing evening.

As I sat there in silence and listened, I tried to understand the days that had passed and what was now being revealed. At the start of the evening unsure to my own unwitting role in his story, by the end of it rocked by what I had learned yet oblivious to the horror that was still to come.

Though unfathomable to some, despite its poverty, before Alvaro's death, Rolando's was a childhood full of joy. His father was the centre of that. His mother had died in childbirth so it left just the two of them. Constant companions, together every minute of the day if they could. Rolando said he used to follow Alvaro around like a loyal dog, tail always wagging.

'Partners for life,' Rolando mumbled to me, the words barely escaping his lips.

Back in those early days they worked together on a fruit stand situated next to the church in Vallegrande, the Bolivian town where they lived. Screaming out 'aguacates, tomates, papaya' to any locals passing by. Pressed up against their splintered fruit stand selling whatever they could to earn enough bolivianos to make it to another day.

Alvaro would talk about how life would change soon, improving not only for them, but for everyone in the town. Little Rolando never doubted a word, although if that day never came, he would have been happy all the same. Still, in this future world maybe he wouldn't be out in the heat screaming 'aguacates' but instead he could go to school, get an education, and be something more.

That was Alvaro's promise, fuelled by events in Cuba. He kept his ear glued to his old pocket radio, eagerly tuning in to the wider world with an almost obsessive curiosity. Young Rolando would watch him, entranced by his passion, following along with all his 'papá's' grand ideas, whatever path they took. And that's exactly what he did when the revolutionaries passed through town in the year of 1966 and Alvaro immediately signed up. Even at the tender age of nine Rolando understood the importance of what his dad was doing and so helped him pack his bags, despite the pain their separation would bring.

Alvaro was recruited to the revolution early. The famous Che Guevara had come to Bolivia in November 1966 under a Uruguayan passport and a fresh identity. A balding man with bank clerk glasses and a sharp suit. Many mirrors away from the bearded warrior in the beret that you find today on the T-shirts and posters. These were all details Rolando found out later in life, however. Pieces of the puzzle he would discover as he burrowed for information in Vallegrande's Guevara Memorial Museum.

At the time he knew nothing. Just that his papá had gone to the jungle to fight for a better world. Whilst he was gone Alvaro had arranged for Rolando to be looked after by the priest of the local church, a nice man called Velasquez. And so Rolando sold his fruits and vegetables outside the church, but now learned the alphabet and stories of the Bible inside the church too, all taught by the gentle priest.

From that time on Rolando didn't see his dad once, though he remained in constant communication. Somehow letters would always arrive, telling him stories of the jungle and their work there. By now he could read so when each letter arrived it was like a message from his new-found God. Nervously he would open them, anxious for the fool's gold within.

'The National Liberation Army of Bolivia', Alvaro called it and he would tell Rolando that he could join soon, once things had settled. Rolando clung to that thought, and at night would kiss a picture of his dad good night, full of pride, dreaming of his own revolutionary adventures.

That's not to say everyone was on board. By now many of the people of the town had turned against Guevara's army and were willingly sharing information with the Bolivian army and by association the CIA, who were also involved. It was all anyone could talk about on the streets, little pockets of people whispering together under the shade of the plazas' palms, afraid to be overheard. No one trusted anyone and nor could Rolando, even with the priest. He just sat with his letters and waited, hoping his dad would be home soon, that they'd win and this new world would begin.

In hindsight everyone from the Bolivian government to the CIA, from Rolando to his poor father, had overestimated the power of this National Liberation Army of Bolivia. After a few surprising early victories, they barely made a scratch. Inconsequential in the annals of time. If it wasn't for

Guevara's name being attached to the whole thing, it would have all been forgotten. Consigned to history as a small-scale uprising that never had a chance of success, something Rolando could never get past.

How naive they were. How ill prepared. That his 'dear papá' was willing to risk so much despite such limited power. To throw the dice like that.

However instead of targeting his anger towards Alvaro, his true fury was left for another. At the real villain, 'a monster', as he once shouted in an unusual, rage-driven sermon he delivered from the pulpit ten years later. Directed at the man 'who started this failed revolution and dragged so many people like my papá to their death.'

The last letter Rolando received from his father was on June 15th, 1967. In it Alvaro told Rolando how things in the jungle were getting harder. That support was diminishing and they were struggling to forge any alliances with other parties of the left within Bolivia, including Bolivia's Communist Party which was a major blow. Malnutrition was also a problem, as was a lack of resources, but they remained hopeful. Hopeful for this better world, scorn dripping from Rolando's lips as he told me.

On September 26th Rolando got the news Alvaro had been killed. He told me the tears that day were ones 'I could never experience again'. Peppered droplets of anger that burned as they raced down his cheek, the constant stream a never-ending reminder of what had happened.

After that Rolando didn't leave the church for a week. Unable to face the world or to sell his fruit. The only reason he survived, that he was able to make it to the end of the day, was through the kindness of the priest. A man who housed him, clothed him, fed him and looked after the poor bed bound little boy. And there Rolando stayed, his pillow soaked, right until the day the helicopter arrived.

It was the morning of October 10th when Rolando caught sight of it as it zipped its way above the palms. He followed it all the way down with his red raw eyes until it came to an abrupt stop not far from the church. Curious, he edged open his bedroom door and rushed to follow. When he arrived at the helicopter's destination it felt like everyone he knew was there, sprinkled among members of the army and foreign reporters and photographers.

That's when they lifted Guevara's body out. The icon with his long, dishevelled beard and wild, mangy hair. A skinny corpse-like figure in everything but the eyes. Eyes he'd never forget. Eyes that weren't dead. Two light blue ovals, glistening in the morning sun, somehow present despite death.

'Christ-like' people said, murmuring amongst themselves. 'Christ-like', as they took out their scissors and cut locks of his hair.

The comment was a shot to the heart. He had got much closer to the teachings of the church due to his time with the priest, so now to see this man, the reason why his precious father was now dead, given the same name as his dear Lord was too much to bear.

Rolando left the crowd in tears, though unlike the tears of September, these ones were boiled and stewed in a cauldron of fire. A true hatred was born that day, one all his later years at the church could never hide. No forgiveness could ever be shared towards the bearded man time seemed never to forget. No, in that moment he made a vow to himself. A vow that one day he would get vengeance against this dead, broken revolutionary, and if he was unable to, then he would die trying. How that would be, he was not sure, but he believed in the direction of his Lord and that in time a path would reveal itself. And that path finally did reveal itself over 30 years later. The day he met me.

After Alvaro's death, the church was the best route left available to Rolando. He had a real appetite for learning and Velasquez cared for him where his real father could no more. He was soon passing grade after grade at school whilst rising high in the church ranks too. When Velasquez passed twenty years later, Rolando was automatically seen as the natural replacement as the priest of Vallegrande.

'If only papá could see me now.' That was the thought he'd say out loud as he went about his daily routine. Not a sad thought though. No, it was one that chiselled an immovable smile upon his face. One that knew Alvaro was proudly gazing down on him from above.

As to the job itself, it wasn't without its difficulties, however it brought Rolando great warmth. Alongside the normal requirements for this role within the church, the sermons and the ringing of the morning bells, he also provided a service beyond the church walls. Driving out to the local towns and villages, entering people's homes and providing support. Venturing up into the mountains to the local orphanage for games of football. Knees charred by slide tackles on the sand crusted pitches, the air filled with the joys of a child's voice.

It was a good life, interesting and unique, which also included the many trips to neighbouring cities or even further afar for congresses or meetings with other men of the cloth. To Cochabamba, up to Potosi, or even to La Paz. Long bus journeys, exploring a country he had never previously had an opportunity to discover. Witnessing its beauty, from the mountains to the jungles, the old mining towns to the salt flats, wishing his dad could have seen it all too. Yet it was on one of these bus journeys, an overnighter from Cochabamba to Vallegrande, where his story turned.

Rolando had always found buses a beautiful way to see

the country, gazing out the windows at the views beyond, yet on this trip he was restless. Uncomfortable in himself for unknown reasons, so he turned to his comfort blanket and decided to people watch. This was a favourite pastime of his and an important skill for any person of the clergy, as a way to understand their flock. To see disturbances before they occurred, offer help to those who never ask.

Initially his observations did not amount to much as the bus was full of snoring locals, the types he saw on most journeys. Some drunk, some talking, most exhausted from their journey, or a gruelling day's work.

Standing out from the crowd were two young gringos, perhaps twenty years of age. Not a completely unusual sight as tourism in the country was growing, yet to see them on this bus was rare all the same.

One had light sun-kissed cheeks and long messy brown hair, with a red band pulled round his head to hold his locks tight. Brown eyes, strong shoulders, and a determined gaze. His name was Gio, my travelling companion for a month now. He was sat near Rolando dozing in and out of sleep whilst next to him, slouched back in his seat, was a dark-haired lad, straight not curly, with small Trotsky-lite glasses pinched against his nose. That was me.

Rolando watched Gio and me for a while, curious to see where our journey would go. This wait lasted longer than he could however and soon the priest fell into a doze, which only ended as the bus approached Vallegrande at 3am.

By now Gio and I were awake and going from person to person with, Rolando thought, surprisingly good Spanish. Mine was an American sounding accent; Rolando knew that sound from the movies, yet the other, the sleeper, he couldn't place. The Spanish more rounded, fluent.

Rolando watched discreetly from afar, yet when Gio moved near he closed his eyes and pretended to be asleep.

He listened however, and from what he could make out this traveller was asking about places to stay. Neither of them had planned a thing and were hoping to just arrive in town and have a door opened to them.

The joy of the rich white man, he thought with a begrudging smile.

Yet it was in that exact moment, whilst thinking that thought, Rolando's eyes spotted something he was not expecting to see. A book perched on the seat next to where Gio was sat. Stationary, almost goading him – Che Guevara's *Bolivian Diaries.*

A book he'd seen across the country in more bookshops by the day. A book to go with all the T-shirts and the posters and the flags. An image that taunted him wherever he went. And now this boy had it. This boy who waltzed into his hometown expecting people to do his bidding and find him a place to stay, just like Guevara before him. A similar kind of charm and confidence to bend people to his will.

Rolando bit down hard on his lower lip, veins snaking across his forehead, his eyes lit up like firecrackers thrown to the street during Semana Santa. A trauma reborn, pure and scary, terrifying even himself. Here was yet another individual idolising the man who had ruined his life and it was enough to unleash all his control.

Cursing he stared out of the window and found his reflection. He gazed at it, the weary lines running across his brow, the sagging bags hung below his eyes, and it reminded him of the only person it could, and there, in that moment, an idea formed.

When Gio returned to his chair, grumbling because we were still without a room, Rolando quickly intervened.

'It is only small, it is only humble, but I can offer you both a small room. A place to rest your weary eyes.'

As desperate travellers only can, we accepted on the

spot and so the three of us padded our feet down the street, empty but for the few stray dogs, all the way to the church of Vallegrande.

Now Vallegrande was a small town with limited resources, but the church had a surprising beauty to it. A red hue somehow emanating from it, the silhouetted lone tower rising above the palms. And it was into that church we entered, the silent three. There were no words for this hour and Rolando liked it that way. Scared that he might slip his secret, lose his courage, break his vow.

Quietly he showed us to our room. A pint-sized room with twin beds in it, one close to the door, one under the window. Each had a modest wooden table by its side and a firm pillow at its head, with a small picture of Jesus on the cross above where they lay. After showing us the room Rolando then wished us a pleasant sleep.

'Rest and rest well. There will be breakfast waiting in the morning. Now I must go to sleep.'

Both Gio and I crashed down into our beds but where he drifted off, I could not, a state of play I was soon to thank. A light snore bounced from Gio's nose, so knocked out, so out of sorts from the long journey, he did not notice the door of our room creak open about twenty minutes later. Very slowly, inch by inch. Nor did he notice the slit of light reveal a lone eye appearing in the crack. A glint in the dark, followed by more features. A hand, a foot, a head, until the priest of Vallegrande was stood there in the entrance, a white pillow in his hand.

Rolando took another step forward, his heart furious in its cage, then silently glided across the room to crane above the boy who angered him. There, he lifted the pillow to Gio's sleeping mouth and then held it there for an unbearable amount of time. Fingers pinched on the white cotton of the pillowcase, droplets of warm sweat streaming off his forehead upon it. Then he pushed the pillow slowly down and the priest went for my friend's life.

I know this because I watched it, my eyes hidden by the angle of my duvet. I had met Gio a few weeks before on the road and some common interests led us to travel together. A partnership of sorts, only there I was no partner. Instead, I had watched for an inordinate amount of time yet did nothing. No cry, no shout, no movement to show I was awake. Nothing.

See, even though the sight disturbed me, I couldn't say I was scared. The whole time the pillow hung there, I knew all it would take was a call from me and Gio would be awake, and the priest would be in trouble. He was a small man, hunched early, not made for this kind of act. On top of that, we were two, and suffocation was not a quick act so it gave me room to think.

As it was in that crucial moment, the moment to strike, something failed him. Rolando pulled the pillow to his chest, gripped it tight, the white of his knuckles shining in the dark, and then exited the room as slowly as he entered it.

The next morning Gio and I awoke to the ringing of church bells. Slowly we pulled ourselves together, morning dust still caught in our eyes as we wandered out of our little room to find a breakfast laid for us on a great table in the church kitchen. Fresh papaya, huevos rancheros and some freshly made empañadas de queso.

Later, when Rolando opened up to me and told me his story, he revealed it was a spread put on to atone for the guilt from the night before. His way of dealing with his own inner torment. But instead of greeting us there, he instead made himself scarce, and busied himself with activities of the church, delivering a sermon up in the hills, finding solace in the fact he had a reason to leave, a chance to think.

The church stood on a long, winding path that sloped down from the hillside, offering sweeping views of the jungle below. The service that morning was more musical than usual, with local children playing guitars and singing for the congregation. It lifted Rolando's spirits, so much so by the time he returned home, he had nearly forgotten about the previous night – until he walked into the house and found us locked in a game of cards.

On seeing him, Gio immediately invited Rolando to join, and he clearly could not think of how to refuse, his stuttered reply painful to hear. In time though he was glad he joined, or at least that's what it felt like to me as the cards began to fall.

It was clearly a solitary life in the church, always around people but never truly with them. So to spend an evening laughing and joking was something he seemed to enjoy more than he cared to share. And laugh he did, even pulling a joke of his own when he dealt cards for six and when Gio asked why, he replied, a spark in his eye, 'for the Father, the Son, and Holy Ghost.'

But when the laughter died down and we retired to our room, Rolando's mood shifted. His smile faded, and he shuffled back to his bedroom, his footsteps echoing in the quiet of the church. There, he undid his robe, lay down on the hard, unforgiving mattress, and hugged his pillow close. All too aware of the night to come and his eternal vow.

The church was a quiet place as most churches are, scurrying feet and Rolando's loud clanging bells the only common sounds. However the next morning brought fresh noises to the inside of the church walls, sounds Rolando had never heard.

Not that he could understand them. No, the shouts that took place inside the bedroom of the two travellers was in a tongue foreign to his ears. If he did speak English however he would have heard Gio frantically sharing his nightmare from last night. A nightmare that occurred in that room, when he suddenly imagined a figure before him. Standing above him, arching down.

The nightmare was so intense he couldn't move, couldn't even scream for help. Was so paralysed to his bed in an unimaginable dread as the figure loomed down with what looked like a plump feather pillow in his hands. However just as the pillow dusted upon his lips, just as the cotton pressed against the chaffed skin, he had awoken with a burst. He sprang forward into the dark, his heart pounding, only to find the room empty before him.

For a while I played the role of listener, unsure what to say in return. Eventually, when Gio couldn't get past how real it had felt, I then told him what I had seen. Not just that night, but the night before too. That the nightmare was no nightmare, and the kindly priest was not so kindly. That it was all true, yet the first night the priest had failed out of courage, the second caught by Gio's reaction.

This revelation naturally hit Gio hard. Instead of swelling with anger at the priest however, his rage was directed towards me.

That was something Rolando did not realise as he tried to listen at the door. He deduced it was in reference to his actions, but assumed the fury of the argument was towards the man who entered their room at night. The man with intent to kill in a desperate vow for vengeance. The man who got so close to stealing the boy's breath but faltered at the last second.

Instead, Gio tore into me for watching this happen and doing nothing. When he asked how I could do such a thing, I couldn't summon a sufficient response.

Stuttering, I told him, 'I knew Rolando wouldn't do it. I could see it in the whites of his eyes.'

To that Gio slammed a fist against the wall, knocking the small portrait of Jesus off its hook. The glass cracked across the picture as it hit the floor, yet Gio ignored it and instead turned to me, his glare tight. 'That wasn't your dice to roll, Dylan.' He began to stuff his clothes into his bag, socks slithering out of gaps in the zip. 'I could feel the pillow on my lips, Dylan, I could feel them.'

When Gio stormed out of the door, throwing all his weight against the ageing wood, he accidentally knocked Rolando to the floor in the process. Cuddled in his robes, lame on the cold concrete, Gio looked down on him, stared at him, a million questions on his pillow-dusted lips. The only one he could ask was the most obvious.

'Why?'

Rolando looked up at Gio as I hovered in the background. Quietly, like a tremor of water across a pond, the priest then replied. 'For my papá.'

For Gio, that was the final straw. Didn't understand the reason and now he didn't want to. He charged off without a goodbye, smashing the two grand wooden church doors wide open as he went, before quiet reigned, returning the church to its normal rhythm.

At this point I was also unsure what to do. It had been a whirlwind of a morning, yet I couldn't bring myself to leave.

'For my papá' wasn't enough for me. I needed to know more. So, I offered Rolando my hand, helping the small man to his feet, and asked if he wanted some breakfast. After preparing something light and eating in silence, our eyes met and we talked. For four hours straight, papaya seeds caught in his teeth, he told me this story. When he finally finished, I asked the question that had been gnawing at me.

'Why Gio? Why not me?'

Rolando replied quickly, as if the answer didn't need to be stated. 'Because of his book. Because he was another Che Guevara obsessive visiting this town, with the same kind of entitlement, paying homage to the man that murdered my papá.'

His voice was painfully serious, yet all I could do is laugh.

'Gio?' I asked. 'Gio, a disciple of Guevara?' I reached over and feathered a hand to Rolando's shoulder. 'I'm sorry, but you should have tried to kill me instead. Our Italian friend is no Guevara fan. He has just seen a movie about Che, and it gave him inspiration to travel. The only reason he had the book was because I had given it to him to try educate him further. Gio was just travelling across South America going which way the wind blowed and one day in La Paz, I was that wind. Because I am the actual student of Che, to the tune of academic study.' I had taken a pause, a sip of tea, and then continued.

'I am a travel writer, pitching an article centred on Guevara's status amongst the people of Bolivia in comparison to Cuba and his homeland Argentina, where I am going next. And I hope you don't mind me saying so, but this story is about the finest piece of research I've done yet… if you don't mind me using it?'

Rolando's face shifted from astonishment to shame, realizing he'd nearly broken his vows as a priest to fulfil a childhood promise – a promise he wouldn't have succeeded in keeping because of a careless, nearly fatal mistake.

He looked up at me, and then he cried. He wept, wretchedly, like the nine-year-old boy who had just lost his dad, and I did all I could to comfort him.

As the night drew on, the dying heat of a chamomile tea in my hands, I then told him this attempted killing wasn't holy of him.

In return he straight out quoted me, verbatim, 'Breach for breach, eye for eye, tooth for tooth: as he hath caused a blemish in a man, so shall it be done to him again.' He then drew a long, tortured breath as if he'd been preparing that response his entire life.

I scoffed in return. 'I was raised Catholic, amigo, I know those words and we both know you're missing out the key part Jesus says back. "Whosoever shall smite thee on thy right cheek, turn to him the other also."'

To that Rolando hung his head, shoulders shaking once again.

'Regardless,' I continued, 'you left room for God's wrath and if that's what you wanted, then your God delivered.'

To that Rolando's brow furrowed, so I shared with him some of the history of the continent over the last thirty years. The right-wing dictators, the US interventions, the suppression, the disappearances, and all the terrible murders of people who fought against both the church and state. People 'like his papá'.

Finally, I added, my head lowered, 'I think your old nemesis Che has had his revenge taken on him.'

Rolando nodded slowly, eyes half-closed, as if turning my words over and over in his mind like a stew on the fire. When he finally spoke, his words slipped from his lips as if they weren't meant to reach my ears. 'That wouldn't have made my papá happy.'

I could only nod back, feeling the weight of his sadness. A broken shadow of a man, who then reached out and placed two fingers on my brow, the warmth of the tea spreading from his fingers into me. And there, in that gentle shared moment, we prayed.

'Padre nuestro, que estás en el cielo. Santificado sea tu nombre. Venga tu reino.'

Following our conversation, I returned to my little room, this time with no Gio around to play cards with before bed. Instead, I began to write, spilling every confusing, disturbing, challenging moment onto these pages. Hastily inking it down, dreaming of the article I would soon be pitching to all the magazines. Thinking only of me, my ego soaring at the thought of the awards I could win.

After marking my final full stop, the last pages a struggle due to my own weary eyes, I decided it was time for bed. With little to no rest over the previous two nights, it couldn't come quick enough, and as soon as my head dropped to the pillow I fell into the long, heavy sleep.

My eyes closed, and darkness swirled around me. Little bursts of light flickered, but otherwise, I dreamed of nothing. After a while, the heaviness eased, replaced by a new feeling – a suffocating grip that pinned me to the bed. Paralyzed, unable to move, just like in Gio's nightmare, I tried to scream, but no sound came, which was strange. That's when I noticed a shadowy figure sliding across the floor. They drifted closer, inching toward me until they were leaning over, staring down, their face blurred and lost in the dark. Only then did I see what they held in their hands. Panic rose as I tried to move, to pinch my fingers, bite my tongue, anything to escape the terrifying paralysis, but I couldn't.

All I saw was a rectangle. Four corners, hovering above me, descending lower and lower until they were nearly touching my lips. I could almost taste the fabric, the sweat-stained pillow of a man in distress. And then it hit me, the realization sharp and sudden, and only then did I wake. Right at the last moment, I screamed.

My eyes flew open to find a room bathed in morning light. The sun's warmth creeping underneath the little curtain at the window, to shine across my face. I reached over to look at my watch, confused at the time that shone back at me.

It was well past noon, which was strange because the morning bells had never allowed me to sleep in so late. I sat up in bed, slowly, still disoriented, and that's when I heard it. Another sound that had never echoed within these church walls before.

A sharp, loud bang that pierced the day, its violence permeating through the air, before it echoed ominously off the great church bell. The bell now splattered in liquid, which trickled down its side, before dripping of the lip and painting the church floor crimson red.

Therapy for Therapists

Helping Hearts & Minds
245 San Mateo St
San Francisco, CA

<u>*Client Name:*</u> *Wayne Johnson*

Date: 7 Nov
Start Time: 17:03
End Time: 17:58

<u>*Client's Subjective Concerns/Chief Complaint:*</u>
'I feel bored right now. That's the flat-out truth. I think I always need that something exciting and I ain't sure I got it.' Client noted concerns about his mood, urges to isolate from his romantic partner.

<u>*Clinical Observations:*</u>
Client sat in a hunched position upon the beginning of the session. Client appeared dishevelled, which is unusual and a marked change since last session. Therapist observed client might be under the influence of alcohol as evidenced by his thought process.

<u>*Issues and Stressors Discussed/Session Description:*</u>
Client discussed experiencing increased difficulty with his romantic relationship, following an argument with his romantic partner. Left him feeling dissatisfied in his relationship, exacerbated by appearance of a new individual in his life who seems to show a romantic interest in him, something that has troubled the client.

<u>*Interventions/Methods Provided:*</u>
Discussion of symptoms, more counselling,

identification and exploration of emotions. No medication.

Assessment:
Client's endorsed symptoms and presentation show little signs of depression. Life dissatisfaction is more likely due to the impact of his romantic relationship and the pressure of his job.

Plan:
Client has committed to having productive conversations with romantic partner and not ignoring her needs. Client has also committed to getting more help to reduce the demands and stress of his current job.

Clinician Signature: Michael Walker

This story again. Copy and paste, just with a different client digging their nails into the seat. The middle age dissatisfaction, the pressures of a career, the various strains on a relationship and then bam, the exciting new person magically appears on the scene, and chaos duly follows.

It's almost like I get one every year, invariably always lost males. A tale as old as time and now the serpent is back, Wayne the latest to fall. He'd mentioned this Mia before of course and even from the first time I'd sensed she was someone to note. Over the following sessions Mia continued appearing, each time with a bit more mental weight behind her whilst simultaneously Jazmine, his wife, was talked about more negatively. It was like a set of scales that over time changed balance. As one side comes up, the other goes down. That's just how it was. I knew it better than most, just from the other side.

Wayne has been seeing me for a good five years now,

one of the many too wealthy clients I gave therapy to in and around the Bay. He was different to the rest though. Genuinely likeable which wasn't something I said freely. A client I looked forward to seeing, both gentle and strong. In fact Wayne was a man of opposites. Diminutive with a powerful voice, fierce eyes with a soft heart. He was also black, which was only worth noting because every other client I had was white. With therapy I often found people searched for a therapist that reflected themselves because they thought they might be able to understand their issues and experiences better. Wayne did not think like that despite the fact his old man had links to the Black Panthers, Jazmine worked for a non-profit in Oakland fighting black oppression, whilst Wayne himself aspired to be Mayor of Oakland with a manifesto that aligned with his dad's politics.

We'd bonded quickly, Wayne opening up to me early, baring his soul. Comfortable to tell me things he could never share with Jazmine, which was most obviously apparent now. Trying to help him with this Mia and unlock her train of thought for him, though the psyche of a white woman in her twenties is even more remote to me, and in reality every second I spend talking about Mia, my small, fragile mind is being dragged back to my own Mia-like conundrum. The one that finished with the car crash end of my marriage.

See, for Wayne's Mia, I had Dylan f-ing Jones, the man wonder himself. Only Wayne was in the role of Emily, my wife, and Dylan was Mia and I was poor old Jazmine left on the shelf. I wish it had been the other way round. That I had been in the alpha-Wayne position making all the calls, deciding who to love, but inevitably that was never my card to draw. Born that way. Instead, for me it was Emily and Dylan f-ing Jones popping up in practically every

111

conversation we shared. Dylan, who burst onto the scene at exactly the wrong time in our relationship and wreaked havoc in the kernels of my brain.

Even now, six months later, sessions like this with Wayne bring it all back. Suddenly Dylan's face is right there again, as unavoidable as the rising of the sun. Dylan, with his Ginsburg glasses, his flowing, dark hair and deep blue eyes. Dylan, with his pseudo-celebrity History Channel career and adventurous academic past. Dylan, with just his name, Dylan, which meant a set of parents who combed the hippy fields in the seventies looking for daisies to string round their neck, compared to my accountant bore of a father.

Why he had a thing for my Emily, why he had pursued my wife instead of all the millions of women who no doubt fawned after him, only added to the frustration. It's not like Emily was a knock-out. Sure, she was funny, smart and beautiful in an intelligent kind of way, but I always thought I was the only person who saw that. It's why the whole thing took me so much by surprise and made me act like I did.

It had all kicked off with Emily's new job, as the producer to Dylan's award-winning *Discovering Fidel* show. Just the fact he was presenting a show on Fidel Castro was enough to highlight our stark differences. In one end it was me, Mr Play-by-the Rules with my school pick-ups, my Sudoku before bed and my intermediate Spanish, whilst in the other was Indiana Jones reborn with his books about revolutionaries, his second home on the beaches of Mexico, and his death-defying tales involving murderous priests down in the Bolivian jungle. How does one even compete with that kind of person?

Instead all I could do was moan to Juana, our former nanny, every time his face came on screen. I was able to say all the things to her that I couldn't say to Emily because Juana listened. I felt heard by her which couldn't have been said about Emily, who if she wasn't distracted by Dylan, then she was by her job or by Sam, our little boy. I was a pitiful last on that list.

Last to get any attention, which in the end broke our marriage. Her actions, not mine, which led to the series of unavoidable consequences that put me where I was now. A situation Wayne could be in shortly if he didn't sort things out fast.

Date: 14 Nov
Start Time: 17:02
End Time: 17:59

Client's Subjective Concerns/Chief Complaint:
'It ain't easy being me. Doing what I do. This helps keep my mind off that.' Client shared the stress of his professional life and how he is distracted by new individual in his life.

Clinical Observations:
Client appeared more content this week, more alert and engaged in the session. A new energy and purpose shown by the way he sat in his chair and spoke.

Issues and Stressors Discussed/Session Description:
Less issues and stressors as client discussed how getting extra help in his professional life has helped his romantic life.

Interventions/Methods Provided:
Discussion of symptoms, more counselling, identification and exploration of emotions. No medication.

Assessment:
Client's endorsed symptoms and presentation show

113

little signs of depression. Life dissatisfaction similar to last week, though improvements suggest progress.

Plan:
Client will continue getting help in his work. Client wants to continue conversations with new individual and is convinced that is the right course of action. Therapist does not tell him otherwise.

Clinician Signature: Michael Walker

Wouldn't be good for his mayoral campaign. Disastrous even, especially because of his race, the grim reality of the day. These things always come out in the end, but Wayne knows that. He's a smart man, smarter than me. It's not my job to tell him what to do, I'm just there to listen. To listen and tell him I understand. Other therapists are more direct, like to give advice. Some even give their clients a step-by-step plan of what to do, yet I've always been the gentler type. A nodder. Quiet man they say, but that's only around people I don't know.

Emily used to nag at me to find more friends. That I needed a different outlet as if this was the problem in the relationship and not Dylan f-ing Jones.

'Go out and meet some people,' she'd crow, as if finding male friends in your forties was the easiest thing in the world.

'I've found loads,' she'd brag, ignoring the fact they were all work colleagues or linked to work colleagues whereas I worked alone out of the rented office two miles down the road from where we used to live.

After her pressure became overbearing I gave Bumble meet-ups a go, swiping my way through the city. It just made me depressed. Every single man I saw on there either worked in tech or was into gaming which was the last thing

I wanted. Not my scene. But I wasn't looking for friends anyway, I just wanted my absent wife. That was enough for me and for little Sam too. Not Emily though, especially when I asked her to be home more, for his sake and mine.

'And sacrifice my career,' she'd grunt. 'Everything I've worked at for years, smashing down all these walls around me, to just give up because I've had a baby and now you want me to be a fifties housewife. Is that what you want?'

I wonder how much time she spends with Sam now, considering she got custody. The horrid irony where she got him after all I did to raise him whilst she was busy flirting with Dylan Jones. I barely get to see Sam now, things ended that badly, and when I do there's a distance there which she's clearly manufactured. Another resentment to add to the growing list, especially as if it was the other way around I'd be at his side non-stop. Now I just forlornly remembered all those days in Dolores Park, at the museums, watching the Giants. Memories he's likely forgot.

Date: 21 Nov
Start Time: 17:04
End Time: 17:58

<u>*Client's Subjective Concerns/Chief Complaint:*</u>
'This isn't how I thought it would go. We were like one person once, but these days I can't be dealing with her.' Client returned to his dissatisfaction in his romantic relationship, though it did not get him as down as before.

<u>*Clinical Observations:*</u>
Client appeared energised, with greater purpose, even though his romantic relationship is under duress. New individual in his life has had a clear impact, alongside growing success of his professional life.

Issues and Stressors Discussed/Session Description:
Client discussed how his romantic relationship is struggling.

Interventions/Methods Provided:
Discussion of symptoms, more counselling, identification and exploration of emotions. No medication.

Assessment:
Client's endorsed symptoms and presentation show little signs of depression. Life dissatisfaction is more likely due to the impact of his romantic relationship.

Plan:
Client will continue getting help in his work. Client wants to continue conversations with new individual and is convinced that is right course of action. Therapist does not tell him otherwise.

Clinician Signature: Michael Walker

Walking out of the session an emptiness hugs me. Hollow at the way he talks about Jazmine because were those the same, sad words Emily used too? Did she also feel turned off to come home and see me in slacks putting the kids to bed? Did she feel annoyed when I painted the sink in beard hair? Did she feel unhappy when she realised this was her future, forever?

Every word Wayne says about Jazmine just cuts deep as it brings it all back. How small I felt, how little. How it forced me to retreat further back into my clamped, little shell. A shell I couldn't seem to break from, which Jazmine must now be locked inside too.

I almost wish I could get in touch with her to talk her through what she's going through right now instead of listening to Wayne mutilate me unknowingly. It's practically impossible to keep the lips clamped. At times my listening persona breaks and I bark back. Can't help myself. It's too personal now. Even more problematic, my questions are loaded, not the innocent therapist I'm meant to be.

'How do you think that makes Jazmine feel when you do that, Wayne? Would something with Mia be real, long-lasting, like you have now? Do you think Jazmine deserves this?'

Questions I never should be asking but I can't help myself. As if pushing him back to Jazmine might bring Emily back to me. And when Wayne replies there is guilt there but also a confidence in his actions, a sense of security where he is in complete control and of course I'm jealous of it. Wishing I could have been that type of person instead.

Date: 12 Dec
Start Time: 16:55
End Time: 17:56

Client's Subjective Concerns/Chief Complaint:
'I feel good, alive. First time in a while. No complaints from me, life is on the up.'

Clinical Observations:
Client appeared energised and content with current life situation. Stark improvement from a month prior.

Issues and Stressors Discussed/Session Description:
Client discussed how this new individual in his life was impacting him positively.

Interventions/Methods Provided:
Discussion of symptoms, more counselling, identification and exploration of emotions. No medication.

A few weeks without sessions and I can't believe how much things have escalated. One day Mia was a story, a temptress in his complicated life. Now she's a familiar feature as they're meeting up for a coffee, 'bumping' into each other on the street, messaging every day. All above board but how long before that breaks?

I can tell Wayne is trying to hide his emotions, his lust, even though I should be the one person he can speak openly with. Highlights how careful he is, which deserves respect. Couldn't have got this far up the political chain without it.

He seems a man reborn though. A new zest in the way he carries himself as he shares his thoughts. This is no doubt influenced by his mayoral campaign too. One that's gathering steam at a rapid rate despite the fact he's up against the self-dubbed "White Knight" in the Democrat primaries.

The unbearable Zach Lawrence, with his shiny bright teeth and his endless funds due to his tech start-up. Zach Lawrence with his beautiful house, his obnoxious wealth and his bachelor life. 'The Bruce Wayne of Oakland' they say, yet it's this Wayne who's rising up the polls, not Zach.

It's this Wayne who is bringing in more and more followers to his aggressive socialist platform with a hint of black nationalism to boot. Not overly dissimilar to his dad's

Panther beliefs, he shares proudly. Exactly what this city needs and even though I shouldn't, I tell him I agree.

In return Wayne says, 'That's good to hear, Michael, this city needs more white guys like you.' Then he starts listing off a load of other white guys he likes until it inevitably ends with 'that guy on the History Channel. The one who does loads about Latin American liberation, with the long hair and the hipster glasses. I'd love to meet that guy.'

My throat clams up and even if I wanted to say something, I can't. I just nod like always. Nod, nod, nodding my way into nothingness. The story of me.

Date: 19 Dec
Start Time: 17:04
End Time: 17:59

Client's Subjective Concerns/Chief Complaint:
'Things are good, things are really good.'

Clinical Observations:
Client appears completely turned around from a month prior. Happy with his current life situation, shown by the way he sat in his seat, gestured and smiled.

Issues and Stressors Discussed/Session Description:
Client discussed limited stressors.

Interventions/Methods Provided:
Discussion of symptoms, more counselling, identification and exploration of emotions. No medication.

Assessment:
Client is happy with current life situation even if it is precarious and could quickly fall around him. This does not seem to bother him as he lives day by day, not looking too far ahead.

Messages here, meet ups there. The whole secrecy of an affair even though one hasn't started yet. Just puts a sad mirror up to my life and how depressing it is.

I wasn't born to be the exciting type, to live a life people talked about. Any attempt at that was just a crushing facade. Don't even have to look back far to find an example. The day I pathetically tried to change things and add some spark into my wilting persona and hopefully sweep back Emily in the process. In hindsight the whole thing just looks as painfully naive as it was painful.

I had decided for once in my life to just act. To do something bold and try and gain back some of that control Dylan Jones had stolen. So I'd ordered one of those driverless Ubers because where I was going I wouldn't be driving my Kia back. I was so charged up as I skipped to the entrance to wait. This was my moment. This was how I clawed it all back. My marriage, my self-esteem, heck even my masculinity. This was all now.

The Uber arrived quickly, a Latino called Pedro, and we scooted across the city in a flash. From then on everything was a blur, the whole transaction taking place scarily quickly. One hour later I was gliding out of the car dealership in a bright red Tesla.

Reflecting now it just screams mid-life crisis but back then it felt powerful. Cruising through the hills of San Francisco in a car that made a statement. That said 'I am Michael and I am here. Listen to me.'

In those first few minutes, for the first time in God

knows how long, I felt as if my rocket had launched. That I was worth something and the sensation was electric. Utterly electric, just like my fancy new car. A car I was only able to afford because of all the money Emily was rolling in at her work. And on that note, an even better idea blossomed, because why hit one stone when I can hit two at the same time. If only hindsight were a guidance that appeared in advance.

I had spoken to my car because it could do that now, and it directed me straight to Emily's work for the master plan, arriving just as things were coming to a suspiciously early wrap. Adding logs to that fire, just as I glided into the parking lot I had spied Emily in a conversation with none other than Dylan Jones.

I'd slowly crawled up to them, locked in what looked like a heated conversation. A lovers tiff I deduced. Well, not on my watch, so I whirred down the windows to make my entrance. My big Tesla entrance. Face to face with the man I hated more than any other.

They'd both turned and so I pinched down my shades like I'd seen in the movies so many times. Then, my voice weirdly low, I said, 'Evening, Emily.'

For a second she looked confused. Didn't recognise me or the car. Then the fog cleared and she simply questioned, 'Michael?'

Ignoring her, I went straight for the reason I was there.

'And you must be the famous Dylan Jones,' my tone nonchalant. 'Pleased to meet you.'

I then extended a hand out the window and offered a shake. When it was met I made sure to hold firm and let him know I was no weasel, no pitiful creature who was just going to lie back and let his wife be stolen. Oh no, I was a man. A real man who made bold, exciting moves.

When Dylan finally replied, after breaking free of my

fierce shake, he did so with a question. 'Nice to meet you too. Sorry though, but who are you? Have we met?'

Have we met indeed, Dylan Jones. Only in all my nightmares. But I didn't say any of that of course. Instead I lowered my voice and explained I was Emily's husband, here to surprise her and pick her up from work.

'I'm nowhere near finishing Michael,' Emily interrupted. 'I've got to go back to the office, I can't come home yet.' Then she bent down to my eye level and asked, 'Michael, whose car is this?'

As the explanation rolled out I didn't see any of the admiration I'd hoped for. None of the wide eyes I'd dreamed of for this out of the blue, so unlike me, move. Instead it was just confusion on both her and Dylan Jones's face, which in itself made me confused. So I had rolled quietly away, back to Juana, Sam and Baby Shark.

When Emily finally did make it home later that night she burst into the room and asked, 'What the hell was today all about?'

When I went to reply I suddenly realised I had no idea what to say.

Nasty even to think about, but all memories now. No Emily in my life anymore, no Dylan Jones, no Juana, and barely any Sam. The only thing left is the red Tesla. The one remnant that I can never escape.

Date: 26 Dec
Start Time: 17:00
End Time: 18:05

Client's Subjective Concerns/Chief Complaint:
'I can't think about anything else.' Client is nervous and excited about upcoming meeting with the new individual in his life.

Clinical Observations:
Client appeared agitated this week, perched on the edge of his seat. Anxiety highlighted by the way he played with his wedding ring and rubbed his fingers against each other.

Issues and Stressors Discussed/Session Description:
Client discussed how meeting up with new individual was causing him stress but also excitement and he wasn't sure what that meant.

Interventions/Methods Provided:
Discussion of symptoms, more counselling, identification and exploration of emotions. No medication.

Assessment:
Client seems on edge this week, unsure of himself and what to do. Is fighting an inward battle yet seems determined to continue on with current course.

Plan:
Client has decided to meet with new individual in his life, despite recognising the impact it could have on his romantic relationship and professional life.

Clinician Signature: Michael Walker

So this is it. Wayne, after all our sessions, has made his decision. This Saturday, with Jazmine visiting her parents over the Christmas period, he has been invited round Mia's for a meal. When he shares this, instead of trying to talk him through the whole process and his thoughts and feelings around the event, I just feel dumbstruck. Unable not to compare it to Emily and me, and the whole thing just makes me feel so hollow. Harking back to when it was me, the night the new production kicked off. This time Dylan Jones's, *Who Killed Camilo Cienfuegos?*

The night Emily didn't come home.

I was there waiting for her with Thai takeout but she never arrived. Instead she just sent a message saying, 'So sorry love, everything has overrun. We have kick-off drinks now and then they're putting me up in a hotel. I'll see you tomorrow.' And I knew what that meant.

I read the message on repeat. Again and again and again. And then I had cried because what else could I do? And now Wayne was going to do the same and in truth, it just makes me want to cry all over again.

Date: 2 Jan
Start Time: 17:08

Client's Subjective Concerns/Chief Complaint:
Clinical Observations:
Issues and Stressors Discussed/Session Description:
Interventions/Methods Provided:
Assessment:
Plan:

Clinician Signature:

'I go there, anxious, walking up the stairs to her small, featureless apartment, as if something in my gut was off.' Wayne is reclined back in the leather chair, staring intently as he speaks.

'And Mia is there, dressed up in this slinky, tight fitting orange dress. Her chest out and her smile glistening like some blonde-haired, blue-eyed, Barbie. And I was wowed, struggling to keep my eyes off her, but as we sat and shared a bottle of wine, I finally began to realise there wasn't much more to this Barbie. It suddenly came to me, as if a message from above. I'd rather be back home with Jazmine in her slacks, sat on the couch watching re-runs of *New Girl*, than be here. It's taken me long enough, don't I know it. I've been a bad partner this past month but new year, new me, ain't that right? How could I start this fresh year betraying the woman I love?'

'And sure, I've been tempted, but what was a fling when you had true love and I choose love. Love, love and love some more. I choose love. And so I cut the dinner short and ran all the way back home and waited for my Jazzy to get back. And me and Jazzy are like newlyweds again. Laughing like we've never laughed, fucking like we've never fucked. And it's all just as well,' Wayne continues to tell me, 'because the next day I got a card from Zach Lawrence's team. You know, the White Knight, my closest rival for the primaries. Anyway, all the card said was *waste of money*.'

'See, the whole thing was a dirty, underhand tactic to get me to mess up in the run for the Mayorship and it almost worked God dammit. Mia was never into me. She was a poor pawn being used by that rich white guy probably for crazy amounts of money. The truth of it is she was a challenge sent to me. Not from Zach Lawrence, but from the Lord Himself, and it's a challenge I overcame. I've never been surer of myself and I'm so darn grateful for your help for leading me there.'

He goes on to say that he thinks he's going to win the Democrat Mayoral primary. The polls are looking good, and he thanks me for that too. Wayne then breaks out into that huge, booming laugh of his and he expects me to meet it, but the lips stay shut.

Of course I should feel happy at all this. Happy my client made the right decision. But instead, I feel empty inside because they succeeded where we tore apart. Wayne and Jazmine blossoming where we were trampled. They were better than us, as simple as that. And that hurts, but it also jolts another feeling inside. Shame.

Something I've suppressed for a good while now because previously my actions felt justified. But hearing about Wayne saying no, not only puts a mirror up to Emily but it also puts a big fat mirror up to what I did on that foggy night in October. The one I like to side line. Unimportant alongside Dylan Jones, but now very real and relevant. Because where Wayne decided no, I said yes. Wayne did not step over to the other side, but I did. Cool, popular future-Mayor Wayne shook his head, but awkward me, Michael the therapist, nodded yes. And him telling me all this just takes me straight back to that horrid day when I walked in the front door to find Emily sat on the floor playing with Sam.

'Where's Juana? Why's she not here?' I mumbled, knowing the answer. Wishing I didn't.

Emily snorted in response. 'I was going to ask you the same thing. She called me this morning to say she's quit. That she has to leave suddenly but she can't explain why. I tried to call you but you didn't pick up.'

I felt the colour flush into my cheeks as I mumbled again, 'I was in session with a client. She quit? Like quit, quit?'

'Yes,' Emily replied, a snap to her delivery. 'Did she not tell you this when you drove her back last night? What the fuck happened?'

And that's it. I've never been much of a liar and Emily can read me like a book so why bother hiding it? So, plucking up some courage, I finally told her about how unhappy I've been, about not being heard, and most of all, about Dylan f-ing Jones. Finally let her know I knew all about what she'd been up to and how it had ruined me. How it had eaten me up inside and made me more jealous than I thought possible.

Emily cut me short there. 'Okay, Michael, I'm listening, but how is any of this relevant to Juana?'

I then went back to the night before. That cold, mist-strewn night in October, our last ever date. The night I'd hoped would get our marriage back. To shape my narrative like Wayne, not have someone do it for me. I told her it from the start.

How I had looked up an event for us in the city. How I settled on some live music, the type we used to go to when we were young and in love and laughing, and I put the event in her calendar with no chance to say no. And how that whole morning before I'd been so nervous but also excited to try and pump some energy back into our relationship and finally compete with Dylan Jones. To make our story our own again.

Then I shared how when the night came she was as emotionally unavailable as ever. Polite, kind, friendly but just talking logistics and stuff with Sam and Juana, and when the music started I put my arm round her, just like I used to, yet I had felt her body shudder. And that's when I accepted I'd lost her. That she'd gone and Dylan Jones had won and I was just the crumbs down the side of the sofa. And that thought sat with me as we drove home and then when I drove Juana back to hers, because it was too late for her to get the bus.

Then I told her about how whilst I drove Juana back, I talked to our nanny about how I was feeling, how low I felt, how down, and the whole time Juana had listened. She listened which no one but Juana had done in so, so long. My whole life listening to others, but here was someone who listened to me, who gave me therapy without even knowing it.

And then I took a pause, one breath, maybe two, and

told Emily the final part. Told her how it was all that, the whole emotional attractiveness of Juana listening combined with how low I felt and how crushed I was by Dylan f-ing Jones, that sparked my next action.

'See, when Juana was just about to leave the car I had turned to face her, nose to nose, and then lifted my head gently forward.' Closer and closer until I could fell Juana's nervous, excited breath on my own lips, though I didn't tell Emily that.

'Then I had kissed her. Taking back everything that you, Emily, have stolen from me over the past months.'

I can still remember it now, yearn for it even. Those few seconds when Juana and I were locked in this moment of exhilaration before she roughly pushed me away, no doubt just because she was worried about what problems this would cause, which made sense. Then she had rushed out the car but I didn't mind because I hadn't felt that good in so long. Hadn't felt that alive. A long time ago now.

I finished my story, thinking that was the end of it. That I'd said my piece and all was square now, failing to notice that a fire was now lit in Emily. One I'd never ever seen.

'Our nanny? Our nanny? You kissed Juana. My God, Michael.'

When she finished berating me, when there was no more anger left to give, I decided to fight it. To not back down for once.

'Well, you shouldn't have started this. If it wasn't for you with Dylan in the first place then none of this would have happened. It all stems from you.'

Emily threw back her head and laughed. 'What kind of therapist are you? Like seriously? What do you even teach your clients?'

'I don't teach them, I listen,' I replied quietly.

'Then what is this?'

I took a moment before the tip of a smile touched my lips.

'An eye for an eye,' my words slow. 'Just like the priest in Dylan Jones famous story. The one we've all read, heard and seen a million times over, the insufferable shit that he is.'

Emily sighed. 'For what eye, Michael? Dylan? Dylan Jones. The single most annoying man on the planet – after you that is. Michael, I can't stand Dylan Jones. No one on set can. He's unbearable. The worst. Constantly relaying stories we never ask for. "Oh when I was in the Congo or Mali or Venezuela" or wherever the fuck he goes. Never asking any questions, just telling, telling, telling. The fact that you thought I could be with him just shows how little you know me, Michael? Dylan? I can't even…'

Dumbfounded I didn't know what to say. I convinced myself she was lying because I had to. Then Emily threw me a suitcase and out I went, on the road in my Tesla like I still am now. Heading to the office because I've got nowhere else to go, because that's my home now. And while Wayne snuggles into bed tonight with his Jazmine, the man who dabbled with an affair for God knows how long, I am the one who sleeps alone. And that thought follows me every day as I drive to restaurants in my flash car, gliding down the San Francisco streets. It weighs down on me as I sit down to eat alone once again and replay everything that's happened. As I try to figure out if I'm a fantastic therapist or the absolute worst.

True Colours

From the moment he hoists her, a fresh vitality sparks inside him. His new flag, there, ducking and diving playfully in the wind.

Zach Lawrence watches it quietly, a gently satisfied smile upon his pinched lips. Stationary, as he admires the colours before him. A new vibrancy suddenly apparent at his front door, especially when framed against the reserved San Franciscan sky. That deep set blue and that proud golden yellow, striking when observed in unison with the black flag with its punchy white lettering that flutters next to her. The perfect companion piece. Together they say more about him than words ever could. Symbols proudly hung for all to see, one either side of his spotless white door.

He'd purchased the new flag online from a quaint second-hand store. It had a small rip in it, visible even from ten steps away due to the red stitching they used to mend it, but Zach doesn't mind. He prefers it even, despite the fact it cost more than if new. Another symbol. He had wanted a fresh flag for a while, the black one previously adrift on the left presenting a disappointing lack of symmetry at the front of his home. A lop-sidedness that would destroy a Wes Anderson movie. But no more. Now Wes could sleep easy for his frame was complete. Blue and yellow and black and white, his true colours.

Content, Zach packs his tools away, walks inside and turns the kettle on. The steam rises quickly, seeping its way out of the goose neck as he simultaneously hand grinds a small selection of Ethiopian coffee beans. Ten motions to the left, ten to the right like always. He then drops the grains down on a scale, subtracts a teaspoon away to ensure the proper weight and puts the rest in the V60. To finish he carefully pours the water over in a hypnotic, circular motion to bring the coffee to bloom and listens as it drips down into his old Edith Heath mug. He then takes a deep breath through his nose, the dark roasted scent never boring despite the number of times he's smelt it.

Complete, Zach walks back outside to take a seat on his front porch, this time looking outwards. Before him the tips of the two flags flap into his eyeline and his heart swells at their movements. The energy and drive they bring to what was, he can now admit, a stale front porch, especially when in comparison to some of the beautiful, grand houses that line his street. Houses of history that have lasted centuries. How he'd have loved one of those, yet it had been too hard to justify a four-bed for someone flying solo like him, especially given the political optics of that. In truth he didn't want the extra space. It would have felt too empty, too isolated. Plus Elena, his cleaner, already took too long for his liking as it was. No, this place worked just right for him, particularly now he'd sorted out the front porch.

Comfortably reclined in his Adirondack chair, Zach moves to take the first sip of his coffee, yet it is as it graces his lips a familiar mop of curly, matted brown hair bobs into view and Carter's face appears. A face he first saw now six months ago and has seen nearly every day since. Yes, every single morning as he sits on his porch with his coffee, Carter trundles by. He's been on the street for longer than Zach. 'An old-timer' as other neighbours say, none very fondly, but Zach likes Carter. He's proud to say he makes an effort with him. That they chat and Zach knows what he does with his day because he doesn't think many others do. Certainly not the Johnsons next door. Where they turn away Zach Lawrence says, 'Good morning.'

Carter shouts, 'Hey' in response and gives him a wave.

Coffee in his left hand, Zach moves his right to his brow and salutes.

In return, Carter points to Zach's new flag and says, 'Nice.'

'You like it?' Zach tries to hide his smile.

'Suppose,' Carter replies, neck arching upwards. 'Seen a lot of them around recently. Them too.' He now points to the black one. 'What's next? Pride?'

Zach laughs though at the same time he can't work out the nature of the comment. He's also quite surprised at Carter's social political knowledge though he keeps that thought to himself. 'Just these for now.' He smiles politely. 'Anyway, nice to catch you. See you around.'

Carter nods at this, then asks, 'Where you going?'

'What?'

Carter tilts his chin. 'Just you said, "See you around," so I figured you were off somewhere.'

'Oh no.' Zach laughs awkwardly. 'Just sitting here enjoying my morning coffee.'

'Oh right,' Carter replies, shifting his weight from one leg to the next. 'See you around then.'

He swivels in the street as if unsure where to go despite the fact he appeared to be walking with such purpose just a few moments ago.

Zach says nothing but watches on as the cogs in Carter's mind whir before he spins on his heels and returns in the direction he came from, shuffling forward in an ungainly manner. A grin forms on Zach's lips at this typical show of behaviour. Nothing unusual here, but only because he's seen it all before.

Once Carter is out of sight, he finally takes another sip of his coffee only to find that it's frustratingly lukewarm. This is exactly why he gets coffee in takeaway cups from the local cafe, even when he's sitting in. Helps maintain that optimum temperature for longer, a temperature that has long since been lost from his coffee due to his conversation with Carter.

Zach snaps upright, strides inside, feet dragging over the restored oak floor, and shoves his coffee into the microwave. He's loath to do this as he knows it brings out bitterness but equally he doesn't want to go through the whole process of making a fresh one. When the microwave finally pings he decides to put the porch dreams away, open up the laptop and get to work. Before starting on his emails however he has one last thing to do. Gliding over to the turntable in the corner of the room, Zach unsheathes the *Black Saint and the Sinner Lady* LP inside its sleeve, lifts the needle and slowly lowers it down onto the spinning vinyl. After a brief glitch the sound kicks in and Mingus's bass jumps into life. Now he is ready.

Sixty-seven emails await Zach which he considers a pleasantly low amount, especially considering some of the other mornings he's faced recently. That's what starting a company entails. People always wanting him, needing him and even though he's sold off lots of the business to concentrate on his aspiring political career, he still likes to maintain an element of control. To run an eye over every outward facing communication, to be let in on even the smaller structural decisions. As Zach sees it, all founders are built that way. People wouldn't let strangers bring up their baby, so why would he cede control of his? One he's loved and nurtured for far longer than most parents. An idea that he'd had since college that got laughed away until it became one of the buzzwords in the city, the name on everyone's lips.

With that thought Zach gets to work yet loses track of time in his emails and it's only when his stomach starts to gurgle he realises it's time for a break. He takes a sip of water, switches his Slack to away, and goes to get some lunch. It's as he's on route to the cafe, a small Italian one that makes some of the best salads in the city, that Zach sees Carter again.

He waves at Zach, this time from across the street and yells, 'Where are you going?'

'Just for some lunch,' Zach shouts.

'Nice,' Carter replies before leaving an unnaturally long pause in the air.

They both then stand there in silence, smiling at one another before Zach shouts, 'Nice to see you, man. See you around.' He then waves sharply, turns in the direction of the café, and hurries his way down the street.

When the salad arrives it's as delicious as ever and Zach decides to eat in, thinking that more time spent there might reduce the possibility of another Carter exchange that day. Not that he doesn't like Carter, in fact he cherishes their relationship and has told lots of people all about the friendship. Just today he doesn't have the energy for it.

Yesterday he didn't either, mind you, but life has been busy for him recently with the handover, not to mention his bid to become the Democratic candidate for Mayor of Oakland. Running on a campaign to bring financial aid to those who need it most, using the capabilities of his own tech business to be able to zone in on the most important areas to target. His campaign is only getting started and the candidate he is up against, Wayne Johnson, is in the ascendancy, but it's given Zach a drive like he hasn't had in a long time. Others have noticed it too. That spring in his step as he hosts numerous events across the city to publicise his work to help the poor. LinkedIn and X were so abuzz when he launched his campaign that he doesn't doubt he'll eventually succeed, because that's what he does. Succeed. Even if it takes time, he knows he'll get there one day.

This time on the walk home Zach doesn't see Carter but he does see his flags, jumping out long before he gets to his house. Blue, yellow, black and white, his colours now. Zach gazes up at them as he hops up the stairs to his front door. Then it's right back to another freshly brewed coffee, right back to Charles Mingus and right back to emails and his work.

By the time evening comes around Zach has not only replied to everything, but he's also had three meetings, spoken on one podcast about his mayoral campaign, and fine-tuned a junior marketing employee's blog post. He feels a certain satisfaction with a day well done as he pours a glass of Cabernet Sauvignon, one directly from the Dominus Estate, his favourite Napa producer and a bottle he enjoys weekly, then he returns to his porch to enjoy the early evening.

Bringing a blanket to his shoulders for the growing cold, Zach sits on his Adirondack and enjoys the setting sun that has managed to find its way out of the grey. A purple hue that gives the flags even greater vibrancy. A late day spectacle that brings his day to a pleasant close.

After dinner, takeaway ordered from the new Pho restaurant that has opened four blocks away, he begins to wind down for the night. This follows the normal routine of a few chapters of his latest non-fiction book followed by a quick name scroll on LinkedIn and X to make sure everything is in order, before he turns out the lights ready for another 5:00am rise.

Only Zach's sleep is disturbed that night. Maybe it's the wind that fights at his windows, seeping from the crevices, encouraging him to pull his blanket tight, or maybe it's the noise at 1:17am. The banging and crashing from the front of his house that he's too anxious to confront. Whatever it is, sleep only comes when Zach's body can't resist another second and he crashes into a deep slumber that is only broken by the bleeping of his emergency alarm at 6:45am.

Groggy, Zach rises and makes his way to the kitchen to start his day with a coffee. A strong one to shake off the night's unrest. Only when it's done does he make his way to the porch, yet it's straight as Zach opens the door that he notices what's happened.

The flag is gone.

The black one remains, but gone is the blue and yellow. Up just a day and already vanished. Staring up at the open empty space, shock hits him. He's never had anything stolen before and this flag is gone in a blink. Quickly he takes a glance to see if it's fallen or blown away before it dawns on him someone must have taken it. Probably because they're in opposition to it, to what it stands for. That's why it's gone.

Immediately Zach grabs his phone, takes a quick snap of the empty pole and uploads a post to his socials. He then crashes down into his Adirondack, brings his coffee to his lips and scrolls through the responses. Only now the coffee tastes bitter to him and it puts him in a foul mood. So much so that when he finishes the last brown swirl to find Edith Heath's perfectly glazed ceramic base below, Zach heads back inside to get on with his day. Too late to cross paths with Carter this morning, so it means he can go straight into his routine. Laptop open, Miles Davis now on the record player, Italian cafe again for lunch. Yet it's as Zach is heading to the cafe his routine changes, because that's when he sees it.

His flag.

The jump of blue and yellow catches Zach's eye even from a distance. There, on the other side of the road, strewn out across the pavement. His flag and he knows it's his because the red stitching is there, jumping out like little drops of blood. But it's only as Zach gets closer that he notices the flag has something underneath it. Not just something, someone. His flag wrapped around the shoulders of an individual and of course there's only one individual it could be. Zach knows that familiar mop of curly matted brown hair anywhere.

'Carter. Carter.'

No response. Nothing. No acknowledgement of his presence so Zach reaches down and grabs his shoulder and roughly spins Carter towards him, awakening him from what Zach now realises was a deep sleep.

'Carter, it's me. Carter. What are you doing with my flag?'

Only now does Carter turn to look at him, rubbing his bloodshot eyes with both hands. When he replies it is not the answer Zach expects. 'Are you talking to me?'

'Of course I'm talking to you. Who else could I be talking to?' Zach barks.

'Dunno.' Carter shrugs in return. 'Just my name's not Carter. It's Curtis.'

Surprised, Zach takes a second to recalibrate, yet the anger still seeps through. 'Carter, Curtis. The point is that's my flag.'

'Not the point though, is it?' Curtis looks at him disappointingly. 'My name's Curtis. I don't call you Clive.'

'Who is Clive,' Zach snorts. 'My name's Zach.'

'Exactly,' Curtis replies with yet another shrug. 'Who's Carter?'

Zach takes a deep sigh. 'Well, Curtis, then I'm sorry. I work with lots of people, lots of names. Regardless, the point is that's my flag.'

Curtis gazes down at the flag settled across his chest. 'Yeah.' He takes a sigh. 'Sorry for taking it.' Then he returns to silence forcing Zach to break it.

'Haven't you anything else to say?'

Curtis shrugs again. 'Just it was freezing out last night and my sleeping bag got soaked the night before in the rain. I just needed something for a night, even if the flag doesn't do much.' He pauses. 'Well, maybe another night too, 'cause it's cold again today and my bag won't dry. When my bag is dry I'll give it back. I'll even hang it back up for you.'

'What, no. It's my property. You stole it.'

'You were asleep though.' Curtis now perches upright on his elbows. 'I would've asked otherwise, though I figured you would have said yes, what with your mayoral campaign and all you stand for.'

Again, Zach is surprised by Curtis's current affairs knowledge. Startled even that he knows who Zach is outside the intimacy of the street, yet what he says gives Zach room to reflect. He realises Curtis has touched upon a pertinent point, albeit a different one from the one he intended.

'You're right, Curtis. Sorry. Thanks for not waking me and yes, you can keep it. Just return it when you're ready and let me know if you need anything else.'

Curtis's smile brightens at this and he puts a hand on Zach's shoulder. 'Nice. It ain't easy out here on the street, so thanks. I won't forget it.'

'I understand... more than most round here.' Zach winks. Then, as he's getting ready to leave, he pops a final question.

'Hey, Carter, would you mind if I took a photo of you? Would be good for awareness purposes. To show what people like you are going through and highlight what we want to achieve with the campaign. Is that okay?'

Curtis frowns. 'Rather not. Prefer to stay off-grid, safer that way. Next thing you know people will be moving me along, especially with your profile.'

Zach tries to hide his disappointment. 'Oh right. Of course, that makes sense.'

'Sorry.'

'It's all good,' Zach mumbles. 'Anyway, I'd better get back to work. See you around Ca... Curtis.'

'Yeah, see you around.' Curtis nods as he replies and then lies back on the kerb, pulling the flag over his eyes to return to his midday sleep.

Zach turns to walk away yet not before taking out his phone and snapping a quick photo. When he arrives home the empty flagpole is glaring. Ugly. He tries to ignore it and return to his routine, to his coffee, to his vinyl collection, but he can't. So, this time instead of loading up his emails Zach flicks on his phone and make an anonymous call. Then he goes on LinkedIn.

The next morning Zach enters his day with a zest in his step. When he walks outside to sit on his porch with his perfectly brewed coffee, he is happy to see the two flags back together, once again flapping playfully in the wind. He brings the mug to his lips and this time no one interrupts him so Zach can sip his coffee down hot. Just how he likes it.

Cleaning Teslas

Wash, rinse, repeat. Wash, rinse, repeat. Arms flexed, biceps tense. You press down and you wipe. Scrubbing away the dirt, the grime, the dust. The dark. Everything you wished you could scrub away inside of yourself, but you can't. Only on cars. High quality cars of the rich men and women of The Bay. Expensive electric cars that couldn't even work in your country but speed the roads violently here. Always shining, always glistening, especially after you've been to work.

Sometimes the owners tip, sometimes they don't, sometimes they buy you something from the store. It's harder now no one carries cash. Only the tip is what you rely on, the money you need to save to get you back home, because that's all you can think of these days. To get back to Guatemala. To your country, your people and your little brother José rotting in his cell. To the country Americans are scared to visit even though this country, the land of the free, has had nearly three hundred school shootings in the last ten years and your dangerous, violent, no-go-country has had none. Zero.

But home is the new Wild West and this country is developed. At least that's what they say whilst you just count down the days until you can return. Back to your black sand beach with the swaying palms and the mangroves and the coconuts and the mangoes falling from the trees and the fresh fish caught that morning and the cervezas outside the tiendas and the laughter on the streets. The smiles and the warmth of your people, not this fake Californian niceness that makes you feel hollow inside.

But to do all that, to get back home, you need money, because that's the reason you came, why you made that trip you try your best to forget. Bodies packed above you and below. Some alive, some dead. Hidden in a truck compartment for days on end to make it over the border to this strange land where the only people who really talk to you are the people who speak your tongue. But you didn't come for gringo friends. Instead you came to work and to graft and do everything they say you should to live the American dream, a phrase that makes no sense, but you did it anyway. You worked your way up the country, from LA to San Diego to San Francisco, briefly into Oakland, and now into San Rafael.

The first months nearly broke you, but you expected that. You could do hard. From pot cleaner to gardener, you did your best. Not saving much, but at least opening doors. And then you became a nanny, the one job you truly loved where you couldn't believe what they paid. More in thirty minutes than you'd receive for a day's work back home. All for something that everyone did for favours or for free there anyway. And then you really began to save, to put money in the bank. Saving, saving, saving in the most expensive city in the world. Not that you lived there but you worked there, taking the bus from San Jose up into the Mission. An area full of people from home alongside white people who paid crazy amounts to stand by their side and call it culture.

And it was there with a gringo family the bills vanished. Pocketing more and more until you could almost touch home. Nearly enough saved to build something liveable for your family on your abuelo's empty land. Not that you had much family left with Papá and Mamá both gone and your little brother José in his cell, but that didn't mean one day you wouldn't have a new family of your own. That's what you want and Julio always said he would wait for you and you still believe him even though you know he hits the parties hard. It's the dream that loops like a cassette on

141

rewind, the one that keeps you alive. The dream that had become more of a reality as you took on hour after hour after hour until it was so painfully close, there, dusting the tips of your stubby little fingers, right until the moment it happened. The moment you can never wash, rinse and scrub away.

You were in a car which makes it even more depressing that you work at a car wash now. His car, one you had been in so many times. Of course a show-off red Tesla like all the other road dominating, dick swinging Tesla men. Despite that, he was a nice man at the start. Smiling, a bit goofy, interested in your life. A good papá to his boy and a therapist too which made him sound clever, though everyone's a therapist out here. Everyone's got problems, everyone's got trauma and everyone's got a therapist. Everyone but you because no real people can afford that even though you probably need it most because of your papá, your little brother is in prison, and that night in your employer's car.

It happened right at the end of a drive back to San Jose, like the last pages of a horror novel. You'd been looking after his little boy because Michael was at a concert with Emily, his wife, on one of those organised date nights to try and save a marriage that was falling apart. Not that anyone had told you but you had seen it all with your wide, deer eyes. The growing resentments, the arguments, the tiredness over being parents, the jealousy over her relationship with the TV guy. All of it heating up, up, up before burning black under the flame like a tortilla left on a comal too long. And that night you could sense the date had gone bad. Had seen the resigned, defeated look in his sad eyes. The short, monosyllabic sentences, different to the normal friendly Michael as he drove you to your place. Your dark, overpriced one-bedroom condo with its small windows and cold walls which you couldn't believe

142

because you always thought California was meant to be the sunny state, not a carpet of fog. Just before you arrived however, Michael suddenly jolted out of his misery, a spark reborn and you soon found out that spark was you.

He pulled up slowly to the street where you lived, edging into a parking space under the dark of a London Plane tree that sat outside your house. Then he started to ask questions, being nice and friendly again and you were happy because you liked Michael. You enjoyed his company and being nanny to Sam, so you weren't ready when he lunged like every shit stereotype you'd seen in the TV shows. The dad and the nanny. The husband and the immigrant desperate for a visa.

You felt the bristles of his beard scratch against your face before you felt his tongue. A warning sign, an alert to your body of what was coming. Big and sloppy and wet and you were horrified which surprised you as guiltily you'd always found him kind of attractive but now he was here you felt repulsed. Sick at him, sick for Emily, and sick for little Sam. But you couldn't move, couldn't react, couldn't respond, you could only take it.

Sat there on the sweating vegan leather of his stupid Tesla as his tongue lunged into you again and again like a line searching for fish. For its prey.

Only you weren't prepared to give him that and after the longest few seconds of your life, which is surprising considering every other shit you've been through, you found the strength to lift both hands up, plant them on his chest and roughly push him away.

At first he looked confused and then his face changed as if he understood, but there was no remorse there. Instead it was as if the reason you said 'no' was for all the other reasons you couldn't do it, but not because you felt ruined. ¿Because how could a poor, short, broad-shouldered

Guatemala girl feel sick being kissed by a rich Tesla-owning therapist like him?

But sick you were as you pushed the fancy button to lift the Tesla's door and then dart out before another word could be shared. You shot up to your room, your small, dark, little room, and fell face first into your pillow and cried.

Cried not just for him and for what happened but also because what it meant. About how there was no going back now. How your dream job was done. Gone. You could never face Michael again, but also Emily and little Sam, and more, it had rocked your faith in the whole idea of being a nanny. That the films and the clichés were all true which turned you sour, ¿because maybe that's how everyone saw you? The immigrant nanny who fucks the dad on the sly even though you're not that person and never could be.

The next day you called Emily and told her you were resigning, then you packed up your bags, moved out of your flat and made your way north again.

First you went to Oakland, but after the 'White Knight' surprised everyone and won the mayorship there, that wasn't a place for you. So instead you went over this bridge, this time settling in the county of Marin. Here there were more Guatemalans and community and even a Guatemalan restaurant near where you lived, though the prices were ten times what you'd find at home.

For your first few months there, though, things were good. You found a room with a family who also led you to a job at a local car wash which you didn't like, but you didn't hate either. It was good enough, a place to earn before you could finally make your way home and so you were happy. The car wash didn't pay as well as the nanny job, nowhere near, but it was steady and it was easy and the sun shone most days which was different from San Francisco and reminded you of home.

There was a group of you who did it. Guatemalans, Mexicans, an El Salvadorian, with a gringo in charge. You had fun as a crew, helping each other out, covering each other's backs, some with the same goal as you, others building their life out here hoping for something better for their hijos.

Maybe that's why you wanted to go home so much. Because you didn't have hijos here and all you could think about was yourself, your own needs and how much happier you were back there where the pace of life moved to the gentle rock of the hammock. No gringo hustle down at the beach, though your brother told you that was changing in his calls to you from his cell. A smuggled phone for late night calls with his sister, relaying his story of what happened on the beach. The history of your countries in a nutshell.

What José did you supported, especially after what happened with Michael. An eye for an eye as they say, only you wouldn't be taking Michael's eye too because you'd cut all ties and vanished from his life.

You often wondered if Emily and his relationship survived it. You hoped it did, for little Sam's sake, yet it was something you accepted you would never find out. Right until now. This moment when the car window buzzes its way down and Michael's face is suddenly there once again. Close. Smiling right at you, his horrid tongue flopping about between his shiny teeth.

It is a Tuesday. The heat aches confrontationally, as if it knows what is to come. To fight it Eddie plays around with the hose of the car wash, spraying you all down under the blaze of the sun whilst you wait for more cars to arrive. Laughing and joking as the little droplets of water fall upon you, covering your sweat stained face and the white T-shirt underneath. The T-shirt you wish you never wore.

You don't notice the red Tesla when it pulls in. They are so common round here so it's normal to see a few each day, even red ones. Watching it glide forwards in a silent buzz sparks no alarms and quickly you all go to work.

First, Eddie and Ricardo scrub it down before the car goes through the machine. Then the Tesla whirs its way round to you and Gaby to vacuum the inside. You point for the driver to pull the car close to the curb then knock on his window to ask him to unlock. He must have seen you by now, seen you covered in the spray of the hose, all before you know it's him. But then the window glides down and Michael's face is there and instantly you feel shock and then you feel green and vulnerable as you wrap both arms across your chest and the flimsy white T-shirt behind. And there he looks right at you and he smiles.

'Juana,' he says, eyes wide in manufactured surprise. '¿You work here?'

You can't smile back, you won't. All you can do is nod. Then you slink back into the shadow of the shitty shade your boss put up last month. There you stand still, your breath shallower by the second until it's hard to suck any in, and Gaby sees you and comes to your side and asks what's wrong, but you can't even reply. You just say that you're hot and you need a break and ask if Ricardo can cover you for a second.

She says, 'Sí, mi amor,' so that's when you run.

Bolting across the cracking concrete that lines the garage, over the road, weaving through the traffic and right into the Nordstrom on the other side. There you skip up to the ladies department, grab a dress from a rail, and then dodge into the changing room and hide. Waiting for thirty minutes or more until you exit, putting the dress back on the rail because you could never afford anything that nice from here anyway. When you get to the road you scan every direction around to make sure you're in the clear. Then you shuffle back to the car wash where everyone is looking even though they pretend they're not.

Ryan, your boss, promptly storms out and asks where the hell you've been, and you lose an hour's pay. The rest of the day passes in a blur, worried glances over your shoulder, scared he might reappear, but for now he doesn't. Gaby tries to find out what's wrong, but you can't bring yourself to tell her. Feels too degrading. The only person you can tell is José from the dark of his cell, who comforts you, warms you with his words and that even from his damp, shitty cell he's here to help. And then you fall asleep.

That night you dream of cars, but not just any cars. Teslas. You're in a field. A great, big grass field though the grass isn't yellow and dead like it is in California, but green and healthy and full of life like what they say about the South. And you're in the middle of this field when all these Teslas arrive and they start circling you, going round and round and round, the circle getting smaller and smaller with each loop. And they're all pearl white and solid black and silver metallic and deep blue metallic but not red. Just those colours circling and circling until they're so close that you can feel the rush of the wind as they speed past.

Just as they're getting so close you could reach out and touch them, that's when the red one arrives. Only one, joining the circle but standing out, alone, forcing the other ones to all circle wider. And you're scared and terrified because you know this Tesla and so you try to run but you can't because the other cars won't let you. They just keep you there and that's when the panic kicks in. Anxiety they call it here in California but for you it's just fear. The same fear you had when your papá was drinking and you knew what was next.

147

And it's here now but you try to be greater than it. To breath deep and to conquer it, and finally you see that your feet are able to move and you start skating across the field which is no longer green and healthy but yellow and dead just like a Californian summer, and you think you're going to escape. But just as you are, just as you see a gap to make your exit, out the corner of your eye you catch a flash of red and suddenly the red Tesla is there in front of you. It is driving straight at you, head on, but instead of running this time you have found your courage and now you charge straight back at it. You, toes pressing off from the dead grass, against the Tesla, electricity humming like blood sucking mosquitos at sunset. But you're not scared anymore.

You're fierce.

The next morning you get to work early, determined to make up from the lost hours of the day before. You wash, scrub, vacuum faster and harder than you ever have, surprising all your colleagues. Even Ryan notices, little eyes glancing through the window, though of course he won't give you any dollars for it. But you don't mind. You're here to work and work hard. To earn your money and to leave this broken land as soon as you can. Also the work distracts you from thinking about him, though if he does come now you're ready. Almost wanting it to happen so you can say your piece. But he doesn't come that day, nor the next. Teslas do of course, red ones even whose windows whir down in a suspense, but they're never him. For a whole month nothing, yet a leopard can never change its spots, or so the saying goes.

When Michael returns it's a different version from last time. You can see it in the length of his beard, the stain on his shirt, the rough of his hair. When you get to work vacuuming his car this becomes even clearer. Empty coffee cups, cheese puffs stamped into the floor and a pillow stuffed under the seat. The whole time you're cleaning you ignore him. Don't share a word as if he's any other customer, but towards the end it's you who breaks the silence, unable to dance anymore.

'¿Why are you here, Michael?'

'I need to talk to you. I need to.'

Desperation painted over every inch of his unkempt face and for a moment you feel sorry for him, imagining everything he's been through. But then you see the clumps of his unshaven beard and you remember how it felt when they spiked you and all mercy is gone. You decide to let him have his moment and then be done for good.

'Claro, Michael, tell me what you need to tell me.'

And the two of you walk over the road to the cafe, Ricardo covering you yet again whilst Ryan watches on from the window. No doubt calculating everything he's about to deduct.

'Emily left me,' he says and you act surprised even though that was obvious from the moment he rolled down his window. 'I told her about us and what we did and our feelings for each other and why you left and well everything. And it was the final straw, she left me for good. I still see Sam but I'm basically living out of the office and the Tesla while we work things out. I was so lost, not sure of myself, then that day I came here, which was by pure chance by the way, and I saw you and I suddenly knew. That we are meant to be together. That the moment in the Tesla was the end of something corrosive and the start of something beautiful and I've decided that I do want you. I'm sorry I've been distant and not committing but now I'm ready for something between us. I am, Juana. I'm just angry it took me so long to get there.'

The whole time you stay silent because you're so shocked

you can't think of a word to say. Shocked and amused and outraged all at the same time at this clown who just thought he could waltz in and take you like you were some Disney princess counting down the minutes until your white saviour came.

But you don't tell him any of this. You just nod your head silently and thank him for sharing and tell him you need time to think. That he should return next week after you finish your shift at two. To that his face lights up, his imagination on fire and you feel wrong for encouraging him but also you're happy with what you've done because it really does give you time to think. Then you cross back over the road and Michael gets back in his shiny clean, show-off car, his face now a sorry smile of happiness, and drives off.

That night you give your hermano a call and together you decide upon how you should respond. The rest of the week you think it over and by the time the day comes you've made your peace with your plan.

The Tesla rolls in at exactly the minute you asked, as if it had been patiently hiding round the corner waiting until it could skulk for its prey. Michael pays for another wash and clean because the car needs it, then he pulls over at the side and waits for you. Wordlessly you enter his car, the stupid doors purring up instead of out. For a moment you're scared to sit down, remembering what happened last time you were in it.

Then you think of your plan and it gives you enough strength for those fears to melt. And so you tell him to go to a hidden hiking trail up in West Marin, and together you glide away and even you are impressed by how swish the car is. How silent it is as its wheels roll across the concrete before it leaves the buildings behind and already you're zooming into the hills and nature and towards your trail.

150

When you park by the side of a road, towering redwoods all around you, Michael asks if it's 'Safe to leave my baby here' and it's that phrase 'My baby' that removes any doubts over what you're about to do.

You shake a no back and tell him, 'We're not in San Francisco anymore.' Reluctantly he lowers the doors and you start marching through the woods.

Whilst you walk Michael talks like every white man who loves the sound of his own voice. Though this time he's not bragging but he's opening up, telling you about his life, his failures, his marriage, his parents and being a parent and his work, all like he's had it rough, not you. And the whole time you nod along, say 'Yes' and 'No' and 'I understand' as if you're the therapist, not him, and it makes you think how easy this therapist gig is and maybe you should have trained in that and no wonder everyone does it these days.

When he finally reaches the end of his monologue you're back at his car and he takes a deep breath and looks at you. Looks you up and down like he did that night and your eyes dart, your breathing starts to race and you doubt your plan, especially when he takes a step towards you, places a hand on your shoulder, his breath hot and his forehead sweaty.

'Juana, I've missed you.'

Then, only then, do you reach for your phone. You pull it out, your heart thudding, and call who you need, only there's no signal here, something you've never been able to get your head around. Living near the tech capital of the word yet the phone signal is worse than the rural beach village where you grew up. Your fingers can barely hold the phone as Michael looms in closer and suddenly there is a hand on your back sliding its way down the curve of your spine. Lower, lower, lower and all breath stops and you're as paralysed as you were before, but just at that moment your phone sparks into life.

151

Michael's hand immediately jumps off your back as your hermano's face comes into picture on the blurred pixels of your phone. You hand the phone to Michael and slowly he raises it until your little baby brother is looking right at him. Then José begins to talk.

A relentless attack of words, fire in his breath and Michael just stares back whilst his colour drains. Occasionally saying 'Sí, claro, claro,' because his Spanish is passable.

When José finally finishes Michael calmly hands you back the phone and then he reaches into his pocket and pulls out the keys to his shiny red Tesla. He lifts them up, a sob in his throat, and reluctantly drops them down into the palm of your hand. Your fingers smartly clamp around them and you say nothing as you bolt over to the driver side of his car and open the stupid doors. Then you fall into the light vegan leather of the seat and press the button to bring the whole fancy electronic vehicle to life.

Suddenly a dashboard of lights are flashing back at you like the clearing of a throat before a speech. You're not intimidated though. You've watched Michael drive this enough, had studied him as you came here today, so you know what to do. And with that and a light press of your foot on the accelerator, away you go, leaving a confused, expressionless Michael stood alone amongst a sea of redwoods.

Then you snort. You snort and you snigger and then you erupt. Doubled over with a delirious kind of laughter, an uncontrollable satisfaction at the thought of Michael's face as José ordered him to stay away from his hermana. That he had harassed her for far too long, that he'd lost her a dream job, all her money, shifts at her new job and worst of all, he had touched her without her permission.

José had then asked Michael if he knew his story and why he was in prison.

Michael had shaken his head, and even though your hermano is one of the sweetest boys you know, Michael had always been terrified by just the idea of him, of your family, and you used that fear to attack him now.

José had spoken slowly, drawing out each word like a knife from a sheath, 'Let me tell you a story.'

And so José did, the whites in Michael's eyes growing with every passing second. When José finished, he then moved on to what was going to happen next.

How he was going to give his hermana his fancy car, give her the keys now, and let her drive away. Drive wherever she wanted to go and never contact her again. That he was never going to contact the police about it but instead do nothing and return to his little therapist life. And if he did contact the police or tell anyone or cause even the tiniest bit of a problem for his hermana then he, José, was going to make it his lifetime mission to get him. That he might be in a cell but that meant he had connections, not just in Guatemala but in the United States too, and all he had to do was make a call and Michael would be in more trouble than he ever could imagine.

And the whole plan never should have worked in a million years as it was so beyond stupid, but for once in your life the reputation of your home country helped you. The stupid reputation that your beautiful land was a world of death and destruction and this land of school shootings and new Nazis wasn't.

But Michael was stupid. He believed it all even though my brother had no dangerous connections in Guatemala, and none in the United States. Michael never doubted it though, just handed over the keys and away you go, heading home.

Of course you'll sell the car along the way, this thing only works where the rich people live, but that money will be more than you've ever known. Real money to finally build something on your abuelo's land, to try and help get your brother out of jail early, to be in Julio's arms once again and start a new, happy life in the beautiful country you call home.

So you glide smoothly along, through the hillside roads, the redwoods, the rivers and the vineyards, a painting of American happiness before you, lounged back inside your sparkling clean red Tesla which shines brightly under the Californian sun.

Hero's End

It's the light that hits hardest. Couldn't remember what a full day's worth felt like before, but now it all comes back. So much so that you just want to grab it as it streams in through the windows of the camioneta. A bright green and red one that bundles its way down Guatemala's broken roads, direct from the city to the beach. You used to talk to everyone on these long journeys but that was all before. Before that night.

Now you just sit and stare at the light. Face smudged against the window, watching the fumes of the exhaust extinguish under the cool clasp of the midday sun. Sat all alone because no one came to collect you but that's only because you never asked. Juana would have been there in a flash, that's what little sisters are for, but you needed the time. To breathe. Because you don't think you've taken a proper breath in sixteen years. You can't when you're inside, because to breathe means to be free and you haven't been free for a long time.

Ever since those ruined seconds on the beach when the gringo's finger pointed at you and your sentence was sung. A chorus of boos, taunts and jeers. Guilty, guilty, the song of the day. From the foreigners, the police, and those you once considered as friends. People you head back to now, just an hour until you arrive. Nervous to what awaits. Knowing all too well how a small village works and what they still say. The stares and the scorn. A sunset story passed down from one generation to the next. To some you're a hero, or so Juana says. The one who fought the fight when no one else dared. To most however, you're a wretch.

That includes Claudia and your little girl, not that they live at the beach anymore. After what happened they were the ones who had to soak all the abuse because no one could direct it at you. That was the part that hurt the most. Not what you did, because that's a hill you'll die on. The gringo deserved to die, it was just how it then struck them. Claudia lasted a few months before she packed all their things and headed south into El Salvador. You've never heard a word since. No one has, bar her family, and they'd never share a word with you. You never deserved Claudia anyway, that's the honest truth. She was always better, kinder, stronger, whilst you dragged her down into your pit with the late nights, the drink and the drugs. She didn't deserve any of that. You don't deserve a second chance.

She'll have no idea you're even out and you're glad it's that way. To let her live her life without ever having to think of you again. The same can't be said for your little girl but that choice is no longer yours and it's a stamp in the sand you can accept.

Just thirty minutes to go now and already you can spot the differences on the road. You'd make a game of it if it wasn't so easy. A ball of string that never runs out. New apartment blocks, new houses, new restaurants, new hotels. All sprouted out of the dirt while you were away. Makes sense, the world spins fast, but the change takes even you by surprise. Not that you didn't know it was coming, but it's still a shock. The gold miners' new frontier. The kind of thing you would have once cried against, hunched over beers with the boys at Luis's tienda. Ranting your way into the night as you drank your beers using your gringo paid coins.

And of course it hurts now to see it, but you're not the person to fight that fight. It's not yours anymore. You're a stranger who just happened to be born here. A stranger whose stop is called and so jumps off the chicken bus. Feet no longer planting into the sand but bouncing off the newly laid tarmac.

Keeping it all inside, you hoist your bag over your shoulder and start to walk, eyes fidgeting. You feared the reaction you might face when you disembarked but now that you're here you quickly realise you gave yourself too much credit. No one bats an eye because you're nothing now. No one remembers the man who took a life – he's just a story. Instead of this wounding you, that thought gives you peace.

You start to move, one foot after the other at a dazed pace. At first your steps stagger you towards Rosa's, the old muscle memory kicking in, but then you remember she's no longer here. Another piece of the old swept away by the new.

Juana told you old age got her, but you know that's not true. Rosa was born old; she could handle it. It was the change that killed her, and you only wish you'd been by her side to watch the tides change together, just like she was by your side when you were a little boy and needed her protection. Another regret.

That thought finally directs your feet and you're at the cemetery before you know it. Searching among the brightly painted headstones, the tilted crosses and the grand old mausoleums of the wealthy few for her grave. But you can't find her. Back and forth, up and down. You search everywhere but Rosa's last sleeping spot isn't there.

By now the heat's hug is tight but it's not that which sends the drops down your face; it's the stress. Of not being able to find her, to say your thanks. To say goodbye. And it slowly starts to dawn on you that maybe she wasn't ever buried here or in fact anywhere. She didn't have any real family, only your sister and you who kept an eye; and Juana was in the USA when Rosa went and you were in the gutter. So maybe she never got the resting place that she, above any other human in this dirt-crusted town, deserved.

Yet just as you start to accept that fate you spy the one grave you missed, proud on the crest of the hill. The perfect spot, gazing out across a beach you no longer recognise, full of umbrellas and sellers and lovers rolling in the sand.

Beyond that however you finally capture some normality, for the ocean changes for no man. Still there and wild, its rolling peaks littered with afternoon surfers catching their last rides before the sun says its goodbye. The sight warms you and propels you on towards this final grave. Lunging across the cemetery, the dead at your feet, towards it. One made out of care and love, with a headstone for the ages, fresh flowers at its feet. Bougainvillea sprinkled across it which makes you think it might be Rosa's because they were always her favourites.

Panting, you reach it, nervously excited to say your words. Legs bent, you lean forward and then you see the name.

Scott "Scottie" Johnson
Gone too soon
1991 - 2015

Your knees collapse into the sand with a curse and cry for anyone who dares hear, and you fall straight down atop the grave, bougainvillea jabbing and scratching into your tightly drawn skin. Skin that can't remember the fury of the sun, so now burns under its unrelenting squeeze. But that is nothing, nothing, compared to the burn which rages inside.

The perfect spot, the king of the cemetery, all for the man who put you in your cell. A creature worse than you given a true hero's end. No one ever believed what happened that night, not even your friends who found him and you on the beach and saw the poor girl run off screaming – that you took the gringo's life, this 'Scottie' Johnson, because he stole something greater from her.

And now this. No judgement for him, no shame or scorn.

That was all saved for you whilst he rode free. And you can feel that old anger rising inside. An anger you thought you'd lost, now bubbling inside like one of Rosa's old bagre stews cooked on the open flame. And the thought of her again slices you through.

She, the woman who nurtured you, guided you, saved you from your papá, all forgotten. And this gringo, who committed the worst of all the crimes, given a hero's end. And you can't deal with that. It's not fair. You've already suffered enough and he doesn't deserve this.

An eye for an eye, as the Rosa liked to say, revenge never two steps away.

Holding that thought you spy a large, stray rock on the floor, one born in the throes of the sea. You pick it up, lift it high above your head with both hands, only one thought in mind. To bring it down on this fancy gravestone and him who lays below it because that is what is right. What is justice. Yet just as your hand begins to drop, crashing downward in a rekindled ferocity, you catch a figure in the distance. There, bobbling along the beach, the sun's last hello reflecting off her face.

Your sister, hand in hand with her little boy. The boy she called Josito. A name for you. And as your gaze covers them both, the stone drops from your hand and plants its toes into the sand, and you start to run.

You hurtle down the dune onto the beach, kicking up black sand like the spray of a wave until they're a just a football pitch away, and you sprint onwards until finally Juana sees you and first she looks confused and then her face changes into an expression you've never seen in all your days and so you run straight into her, wrapping your arms around both her and the kid and all three of you crash to the sand in a great explosion of joy, and there on nature's bed you rock and roll in each other's embrace, tears splashing together and Juana is laughing and

159

you are laughing and Josito doesn't really know what's going on, doesn't understand the weight of what is happening, but he's laughing and crying too, a body of three, caught together in happiness, and all thoughts of revenge, of justice, have vanished from your body, fallen in the drop of a tear that evaporates in the clutch of the sand for that's not you anymore. This is you.

Ten minutes later you all rise from the sand. Down as three, up as one, Juana peppering you with questions all the way to her new home. Her happy, beautiful place and you're proud of the role you played in her affording it. You walk inside, hearing the hum of air con as she lights up a flame and begins to cook. Bagre stew, just how you like it.

Then Julio walks in. Juana's husband, a friend who left you on the beach but this time he doesn't turn his back and instead holds you tight. Cries into your shoulder in a way men never used to.

Lo siento amigo, lo siento, lo siento.

Unlocked by him, you cry back as you tell him it's all okay, before laughter takes over and lights the evening as you drink down your Sprite and listen to all that's been.

Later that night when everyone has gone to bed you wander out onto the front porch and collapse into one of Don Lazaro's hand-made hammocks. There you sway back and forth under the gentle stroke of the stars and realise you have something to do. Moving secretively even though you're doing nothing wrong, you dart back to the cemetery and to the gringo's spot. His beautiful headstone goading you under the soft glow of the moon. For a few long seconds you stare at it, your fingers twitching, then you turn away. Leaving this mausoleum of the unworthy, because at the end of the day, ¿aren't they all? Through the history of time, murderers, rapists, thieves, and crooks all given a legacy they never deserved. Well, not this new grave.

You pace a few yards in front of the gringo, right to the crest of the dune for the best view any grave could get. One that gazes out onto the beach and to the sea beyond. That will capture every balloon of orange that rises each morning and falls each eve. And there, a perfectly round rock of the ocean clasped in your sweated palm, you knock down a small wooden cross. One you forged using the unbreakable red wood of the mangroves. Trees that were here long before any man and will last so many moons more, now used to make a cross with a simple name carved upon it. One that now stands tall in the grip of the wet sand below, bougainvillea carefully decorating its arms, and you crash down into the black sand next to it and wait for the light to rise.

About the Author

Ben C. Davies is originally from the UK and is now based in California. His work has been featured in numerous publications including *Fiery Scribe Review*, *Unlikely Stories* and *Left Brain Media*, with articles in *Electric Literature*, *Huck* and *Lost*.

He is an editor for the *Ginosko Literary Journal*, a member of the San Francisco Writers Grotto, and is currently completing his debut novel. Beyond his writing, Davies is the co-founder and director of Studio Luce, a Guatemalan writing and artist residency. *And So I Took Their Eye* is his debut book.

Acknowledgements

To everyone who has read this book, or any of my previous ones now lying dusty under my bed, thank you.

To Gill and Martin James, and the team at Bridge House, especially Allison Symes, whose patient and meticulous editing improved this book tenfold: long live indie presses.

To Natàlia Pàimes, for your wonderful cover design and your patience with my endless indecisiveness.

To all my friends who have read my work and encouraged or inspired it in various ways, from Guatemala to the US to the UK, namely: Ryan, for remembering character names from long-forgotten stories and casually referencing them in random conversations, reminding me that maybe there was something memorable there after all; Jon, Kate, Dan, Alex, Amy, and so many more, for your positivity and encouragement over the years; and to Luke and Jack, for always being willing to read what I wrote, even when it was just a 'shitty first draft', and for offering much-needed guidance, support, and encouragement. Simply setting aside the time to read my work meant so much and pushed me to keep going.

To so many members of the Gaddini family for always encouraging my writing, being my biggest cheerleaders, and supporting it in ways you probably don't even realize. Especially to Chris, Nat, Pete, Addy, and Wywy (you're in a book!).

To all the creative, inspiring Crisps I've been fortunate enough to grow up with – grandparents, aunts, uncles, and cousins – but most especially: to Pal, for your endless positivity and encouragement; to Tom, for putting books in my hands throughout my life, possibly the greatest gift one can give; to Mum and Dad, for instilling in me a love of reading from such a young age, from *The Hobbit* to *Moonfleet* and beyond, and for continuing to read, support, and offer feedback now with my own writing; and to Grandma, who will never get to read this book but somehow read my last attempt despite everything you were going through. It meant the world.

To Elio, for the fresh joy you bring to every day and whose arrival in this world pushed me to write again. In some lofty, ego-driven way, I wanted to leave behind something you could one day read and hopefully connect with. However questionable, that desire challenged me to step out of my long-held comfort zone and return to what I love.

And finally, to Katie, the main reason this book exists. On our first date, through gritted teeth, I told you I was a writer in a desperate attempt to impress. Not only did you make me believe it, but you have been there through every draft, offering the best feedback I could ever receive, no matter how hard it was to hear. You push me ever onward to do more with my life, bringing me so much happiness and love. Without you, the pen would have been put down long ago.

Thank you.

Several stories originally appeared in the following publications: 'The Eagle of the Desert' in *MiniMag* on April 28, 2024; 'Teatime at the Cricket' in *Firework Stories* on July 17, 2023; 'Whose Story?' in *Unlikely Stories* on January 24, 2024; 'Dear Babbo' in *The Downtime Review* on April 15, 2024; 'The Haunted Priest' in *The Other Side* on December 3, 2024; 'Therapy for Therapists' in *Malu Zine* on January 15, 2024; 'True Colours' in *Left Brain Media* on January 25, 2024, where it also made the shortlist for their State of It political writing competition; 'Cleaning Teslas' in *Malu Zine* on January 15, 2024; and 'A Hero's End' in *Fiery Scribe Review* on April 24, 2024.

Like to Read More Work Like This?

Then sign up to our mailing list and download our free collection of short stories, *Magnetism*. Sign up now to receive this free e-book and also to find out about all of our new publications and offers.

Sign up here:
http://eepurl.com/gbpdVz

Please Leave a Review

Reviews are so important to writers. Please take the time to review this book. A couple of lines is fine.

Reviews help the book to become more visible to buyers. Retailers will promote books with multiple reviews.

This in turn helps us to sell more books… And then we can afford to publish more books like this one.

Leaving a review is very easy.

Go to https://amzn.to/43CVBtU, scroll down the left-hand side of the Amazon page and click on the 'Write a customer review' button.

Other Publications by Bridge House

Once We Were Heroes
by Henry Lewi

Where do the gods of Olympus do their shopping?

Do the Old Gods live amongst us, and if so where? And which jobs do they do? Where do the Old Gods shop, or do they do it online? Which football clubs do they support? When Angels are sent down to Earth, how do they get home? How did Vampires cope with Lockdown during the pandemic? And finally, are Extra-Terrestrials dangerous, or do they just want to speak to us?

'Henry Lewi writes with confidence and with imagination. The story about the gods moving to North London provided an interesting opportunity to comment on modern times. The Pandemic features in many of the items in the collection.'
(Amazon)

Order from Amazon:

Paperback: ISBN 978-1-914199-82-0
eBook: ISBN 978-1-914199-83-7

Blood and Electricity
by Steven John

'*We took an excursion around the sun again this year, five hundred million miles back to where we started.*' From *A Brief History of Time in Our House*, a story in this collection.

There are no UFOs or extra-terrestrials in this first collection of short stories and flash fiction by Steven John. Blood and Electricity is about the vital currents that flow through and around us, powering our lonely orbits of life. We are all bright stars that appear close to one another when viewed with the naked eye, but the truth is, we're separated by incomprehensible distances.

'This is a tremendous collection of flash fiction. Steven John is a master of words, but also so able to write situations and characters with which we immediately identify.' *(Amazon)*

Order from Amazon:

Paperback: ISBN 978-1-914199-80-6
eBook: ISBN 978-1-914199-81-3

Something Very Human
by Hannah Retallick

This collection takes the reader on a journey through life, from the innocence of young voices to the reflections of those seeking meaning as they look back at the paths they've taken.

Each story captures the very essence of being human. The characters tackle everyday challenges, face inner struggles, navigate familial relationships and friendships, fall in love and out of love, process grief, and reflect on the beautiful fragility of it all.

Something Very Human is the debut short story collection from award-winning writer, Hannah Retallick.

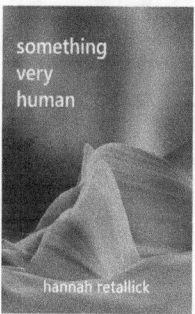

'This was quite a collection of unputdownable short stories. Except I needed to take a break after each one to savour the impact and not move on too quickly!' *(Amazon)*

Order from Amazon:

Paperback: ISBN 978-1-914199-76-9
eBook: ISBN 978-1-914199-77-6